倍斯特出版事業有限公司
Best Publishing Ltd.

U0077368

一次就考到

雅思寫作6.5

雅思 寫作

6.5

暢銷修訂版

柯志儒◎ 著

MP3

運用中西諺語， 寫出高分作文好論點！

收錄雅思寫作常考的【教育】、【社會法律】、【民生生活】時事議題，
一舉攻破申論題的低分圍牆，竄出好分數！

考取雅思寫作高分Steps：

① 抓住考題的核心重點，選定立場與相對應的中西諺語
　► 看【成語閱讀故事】先懂諺語的意涵由來，再延伸至論述中。

② 擬定作文的大綱，運用諺語支持自己的論點
　► 看【寫作技巧解析】、【應試撇步】，掌握作文的起承轉合與高分論點。

③ 直接破題表述自己的觀點，最後做強而有力的總結，輕鬆考到6.5⁺！
　► 按照【作文範例】的模板，寫出令主考官讚嘆的好作文！

　　大多數人考雅思檢定的原因，通常是為了考取海外學術進修的英語能力資格，而其中寫作的部份，與閱讀、聽力及口說等其它考試部分相比，是較能夠經由反覆練習、接觸，來降低考試時的考題變數，並能夠有效拿取高分的重點科目。

　　本書各單元先介紹華語中各經典諺語，並搭配符合其諺語意涵的英文用語，再套用到各單元內討論現今時事議題的範文內，而不論考生在正式考試時對於題目是要採取支持或否定的立場，皆可依循本書中範文的架構，來闡述自身的觀點，並在文內適時搭配較艱深的單字、片語，不僅對於雅思寫作考試有幫助，相信對於整體英語能力的提升，也是有助益的。

　　最後，很高興能夠有機會著作本英語學習書籍，希望藉由有趣的中英文諺語，搭配時事議題，以及各範文有調理的框架及其所帶出的各多元化表達方式，能夠在考生的雅思準備旅程上，提供順風的助力。

柯志儒

Editor

編者序

　　《一次就考到雅思寫作6.5+》甫經出版，有在國外求學或在語言中心準備雅思的讀者紛來沓至，提及這本書補足了課堂中英文寫作教學等無法協助到學習者或考生的部分，很值得捧讀再三。書籍中的範文包含了幾項特點：**「符合學術寫作的要求和字數」**、**「文句通順」**、**「邏輯表達清晰」**、**「論點具說服力」**、**「懂得運用適切的承轉詞」**、**「使用高階但並非冷澀、不常見的字彙」**和**「長難句等各式句型的使用」**，這些都是許多外文系學生或雅思備考考生經過數堂文法和英文寫作課後，在邁向雅思寫作高分的準備過程中需要達到的部分，也是雅思考試中對寫作的核心要求。

　　因考慮到讀者學習習慣等，編輯部與英國籍老師將範文中一些細節部分進行了修正和潤飾並將範文錄音，期許**《一次就考到雅思寫作6.5+ (附英式發音MP3)》**提供給學習者以及滿足仰賴聽力學習的考生，最後祝所有考生都能獲取寫作佳績！

編輯部 敬上

目次 CONTENTS

PART 1 教育

PART 2 社會法律議題

PART3 民生生活

In the past, students in elementary and junior high schools were taught with the same version of textbooks across Taiwan. The national entrance exam for senior high schools was also based on standardized textbooks.

However, as time goes by, today's education system has thrown out the traditional books that were universally used at every school, but has instead taken on a new policy called "One Guideline, Multiple Textbooks." The policy grants schools the liberty of choosing any approved version of textbooks from various publishers.

Instead, the Ministry of Education offers only One Guideline for publishers to adhere to as they design their individual textbooks.

Do you agree with this policy? Or would you rather have the old ways of education under standardized textbooks?

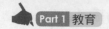

寫作技巧解析

在雅思的寫作考試中，不論考生所選擇的論述為正還是反，評分的重點皆著重在於考生是否能夠清晰地指出自己為何選擇正或反的立場，因此在看到題目後，應盡快選擇自己所要辯證的觀點，並將保貴的時間應用在第二段的支持論點上；而在這個題目中，我選擇反對「一綱多本」的教育政策，並描述在此種升學環境下，學生及家長們常感到「無所適從」，從大方向來看，整體的教育體系讓人感到猶如「the blind leading the blind」一般，沒有人真的搞懂自己在做什麼。

應試撇步

在雅思的寫作考試中，考生除了應盡力展現清晰的邏輯、思維外，也應嘗試將較進階的單字融入寫作中，以示閱卷者自己在語言程度上有一定的掌握，如使用「lurk」這個單字，來形容潛藏在國中畢業前夕的高中入學考試，或是用「hatch」這個單字，來形容學校產生的全新參考書挑選機制，當然別忘了使用本單元介紹，本源自聖經故事的諺語「the blind leading the blind」，形容令人困惑且「無所適從」的「一綱多本」亂象。

 作文範例

 MP3 001

1 教育

2 社會法律議題

3 民生生活

In Taiwan, the educational system has drastically changed from the time of the state-published textbooks to the time of a bewildering array of textbooks. What remains unchanged is the fact that there is still a senior high school exam lurking near the end of junior high, and the pressure is unfortunately the same, if not more, during these two eras. Therefore, I disagree with the practice of "One Guideline, Multiple Textbooks," officially introduced by the Taiwanese government in 1999 and hailed as the polestar by education reformists at the time, who trumpeted the idea of a varied playing field for students.

在台灣，教育體制從原本的單一國立出版教科書，快速演變至今，已有多元、令人眼花撩亂的多種教科書，但不變的仍是潛伏於國中畢業前夕的高中升學考試，以及其所帶來的壓力；所以，我並不認同政府於西元 1999 年開始實行的「一綱多本」政策，即使在當初，這項政策被許多教育改革家號稱為多元教育的指標。

The reasons why I support the traditional way of learning with standardized textbooks can be boiled down to one common theme: the socio-economic environment where the education system is built upon. First, in an Asian society such as Taiwan, the pressure of performing outstandingly on national exams for senior high school is unshakable. In this scenario, students inevitably suffer stress while preparing for those

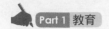

entrance exams, as no boundaries of test materials can be clearly drawn. Secondly, a new kind of mechanism for deciding which published textbooks to go with is hatched, and it has become a commercial one. Schools now have the freedom to choose their own preferred textbooks, and the decisions made can be based upon commercial benefits between schools and publishers, not in the best interests of pupils. This kind of under-table agreements will be particularly prevalent without proper government supervision, and we have not seen relevant counter mechanisms from the government for now.

　　我之所以會支持傳統使用統一標準教科書的教學方式，可總結至一個大方向論點，在於：位在我們所建立的教育體系下的社經環境；首先，在如台灣的亞洲社會裡，要在升學考試中表現亮眼的壓力是無法粉碎的，在此情況下，因為學生無法清楚地歸納出考試範圍，他們在準備考試的過程，將會備感艱辛；第二，學校進而發展出一套新的挑選教科書機制，且是個以商業為導向的機制，因其擁有充分的決定權，可各自挑選偏好的教科書廠商，但學校很可能著眼於廠商私下所保證的個人商業利益，而犧牲了學生的普遍權益，尤其當政府未盡到應盡的責任監督時，檯面下的交易更是普遍，至今政府也尚未推出有效的防治機制。

The points mentioned above lead me towards the standpoint of non-supporting of the "One Guideline, Multiple Textbooks" policy. It is the social and economic reasons that constitute my supporting argument for standardized textbooks, as the newer policy risks creating an environment that is potentially blind leading the blind, where the key decision might not be made in student's best interests.

以上所提及的論點，是我反對「一綱多本」的原因，也正是因為我們現處的社經環境，使我支持傳統標準、單一化的教科書體制，要不然在「一綱多本」的政策下，大家將無所適從，且學生的權益也將有可能被犧牲。

1 教育

2 社會法律議題

3 民生生活

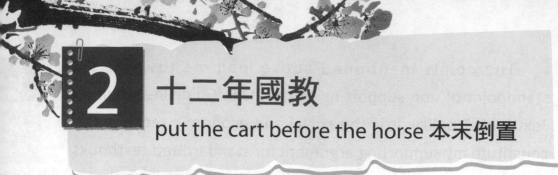

2 十二年國教

put the cart before the horse 本末倒置

成語閱讀故事

　　「本末倒置」所指的是對於事情的輕重緩急不分，出處可追溯至宋代朱熹，在寫給朋友呂伯恭的書信中提到「昨所獻疑，本末倒置之病，明者已先悟其失。」，所探討的即是在事物優先順序的安排上，因偏差而承受了不必要的損失及影響；而英文也有一句有趣的諺語，其意思正好與「本末倒置」相呼應，叫作「put the cart before the horse」，字面上的意思為將貨車放置在馬前，變為無法前進的貨車拉馬，而不是理所當然的馬拉貨車，此種「本末倒置」的情事，對於任何情況皆是無助益的。

In Taiwan, it had been years of practice for students to mandatorily attend a combined 9 years of elementary and junior high schools for education.

However, since 2014, the government has passed the motion to implement what is called "12-Year Compulsory Education," expanding the span from 9 to 12 years. The policy incorporates the 3 years required to garner senior high diplomas into the timeline of basic education, and trumpets continued and a fairer chance at education for students across varied social rankings.

The policy believes that by providing an all-inclusive, compulsory educational environment for an extended 3 years, the gap between students from families at different ends of the economic spectrum will narrow.

Are you in agreement of this statement, or not? Please explain your stance.

1 教育

2 社會法律議題

3 民生生活

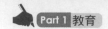

寫作技巧解析

　　題目說道「12 年國民基本教育」將原本不屬於基本教育範圍的高中職三年，編入為強制選項，並期望能夠藉由教育的延長，讓許多國中畢業後就停止受教育的孩子，因為政府所提供的教育機會，而有翻轉的契機；以下範例將採取反對的立場，並批評 12 年國教對於縮小國家社經階層的落差，其所採取的措施，並未精確診斷出現有問題的癥結點，可謂「本末倒置」、「put the cart before the horse」，僅是治標不治本。

應試撇步

　　在雅思的寫作考試中，作文的第一段應先以簡短、重點式介紹的方式，敘述當前所探討的議題為何，而換句話說就是個好用的技巧，可將題目的問題，用不同的文法及同義詞來表達相同的意思，最後再表明自己對於問題的立場，就會是個以開門見山法開場的標準學術寫作。

 作文範例　　　　　　　　　　　　　 MP3 002

　　As the education system had for years mandated Taiwan's youngsters go through 9 years of successive elementary and junior high education that are compulsory, a certain kind of landscape had been developed not only for the receiving end, namely the students and parents, but also for the supporting end of education, such as teachers and cram school operators. Naturally, this landscape can be easily upended by the introduction of any given system, and the "12-Year Compulsory Education" is no exception. The advent of the 12-year policy is based on the belief that by providing the extra 3 years of education, students who would have likely gone stray could have a better chance at staying on a socially accepted course. While there are undoubtedly other facets to this policy, I specifically disagree with the alleged effectiveness of how quickly the system can reverse the strayed youngster rate, not to mention the possibility for this 12-year policy to narrow societal gaps amongst the student body.

　　多年來，我們的教育系統已要求台灣的學子們必須接受 9 年的小學及國中教育，而長久下來，不論是從教育接受者的角度，如學生及家長，或是教育提供者的角度，如教師及補教業，皆已發展出一套合宜的應對方案，而任一新引進的系統，都必將造成相當程度的震撼，這也正是「12 年國民基本教育」所帶來的，而 12 年國教的誕生，是希望藉由提供這多餘的 3 年，使原本國中畢業後

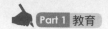
即停止受教育的學生，有更多的機會能夠在社會正途上發展；當然，12 年國教有許多不同的面向，但單就其所期望能夠反轉青年步上歧途的機率，我是持反對立場的，更不用說進而縮小學員全體間社經背景的落差，我是持反對立場的。

First, the former 9-year policy had been adapting while reinventing itself to suit opinions voiced from those who themselves have undergone the 9-year system, and knew where the system needed fixing to better accommodate the increasingly diversely-inclined student body. Over the years, the system had actually morphed into something where the once highly-held academic subjects were caught up by the growing popularity of vocational skills and experiences. In other words, the original system had created a space where students that are differently inclined can all find places to further their interests, either academic or vocational. The last thing it needed is a new system that brings drastic changes, chaos and confusion. Furthermore, such a claim as stating the extra mandated 3 years of education can narrow social gaps is ungrounded. Not everyone is built to pursue an academic related career path, nor does the society need so. Besides, one of the best ways to learn is through hands-on experiences, and it can be more productive for youngsters, who are in risk of potentially going off course, to enter paid programs for internship than forcing them to stay in school. This way, they learn on the job, and are able to earn income, both of which conducive to a more balanced social structure, and hence more effectively narrow social gaps.

在 9 年國教多年後，不僅傳統所注重的學科為教學重點，近年來蓬勃發展的術科也越來越受到重視，換句話說，原本的體系早已開始提供不同興趣取向的學生們發展的舞台，而他們所最不需要的，即是一個會帶來劇變、混亂及困惑的新體系；此外，12 年國教所倡導的「將高中職 3 年融入義務教育將縮小社經差距」是沒有根據的，不是所有人都適合追求與學術相關的職業，而社會的整體運作也並不需要所有人都追求學術，而若要改善年輕學子誤入歧途的機率，協助他們加入實習計畫，也會比強制他們留在校園內來得有效，這樣一來，他們不僅能在實習工作上學習相關經驗，也能夠賺取相對的報酬，這對於社會結構的平衡及縮小社經差距將更有效果。

Therefore, based off of the two points made above, I disagree with the statement that by introducing "12-Year Compulsory Education," social gaps between students from both ends of the economic spectrum will become smaller. Governments should take a closer look, and decipher through what the root problem that needs fixing. If not, they will only be putting the cart before the horse, where there is not enough momentum push for what is needed forward.

綜合以上兩點，對於有關「12 年國民基本教育」將縮小社經階層兩端差距的說辭，我採取反對的立場，而政府應當仔細過濾、研究出當今教育問題的根本，要不然只是本末倒置、白忙一場，整個社會終究無法有效地進步、發展。

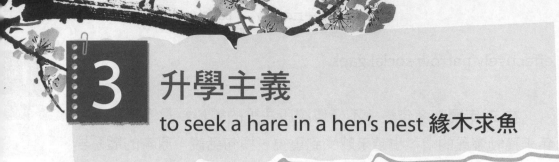

3 升學主義
to seek a hare in a hen's nest 緣木求魚

成語閱讀故事

　　成語「緣木求魚」，字面上的意思為「攀爬到樹上找魚」，比喻的是某人所採取的行動，與想達成的目標相反，並且是沒有關聯的，以致無法達成目標；其出處來自《孟子·梁惠王上》，於戰國時期，孟子為勸說齊宣王不要為了達到稱霸天下的目的，而實行大規模的討伐、佔領等軍事行為，要不然「以若所為，求若所欲，猶緣木而求魚也。」，指的就是齊宣王用錯方法，天下將更為混亂；而在英文中，可用「to seek a hare in a hen's nest」來形容「緣木求魚」，所表達的即是在雞窩裡尋找野兔，不僅浪費時間，且根本用錯方法，無法達成期望及目的。

In Asian countries, education systems put much emphasis on taking exams and how students are able to score higher points. Students are generally required to take national entrance exams to enter senior high schools and colleges, and are assigned to schools solely based on exam scores.

But what strongly drives behind this contorted approach to teaching and learning seems to stem from the society at large. As a whole, the Asian society has a deep-rooted habit of gauging individual worth by which school students go to and the school rankings, which are largely determined by exam scores.

Do you think it is fair to place such heavy weight on taking exams? Or do you think otherwise?

寫作技巧解析

　　題目說道，在多數的亞洲國家中，教育的重點經常放在升學考試上，也就是所謂的「升學主義」，而背後主要的原因，來自於社會總是對於學生及其畢業的學校排名有所連結，進而藉由此連結來評估學生本身的能力，但如此的教學方法是否公平呢？以下寫作範例採反對立場，說明逼迫學生死背、苦讀，是個「緣木求魚 to seek a hare in a hen's nest」的教學方式，並無法在此系統中找到學科考試外的明日之星。

應試撇步

　　雅思的寫作考試，在第一段曉以大義、簡述文章所探討的議題後，即可在第二段展開舉證、論述的動作，以支撐考生自己在第一段結尾時所表達的立場；至於該如何舉證呢？在日常生活中，應注意、觀察身邊所發生的新聞及時事，可將其融入文章論述內，使考生論點的可信度大增，就如在本範文內，引述了明星主廚成功的故事，不僅增加文章趣味，也加強論點。

作文範例

🔵 MP3 003

1 教育

2 社會法律議題

3 民生生活

Schools in Asia are spending a copious amount of time training students to do well on national entrance exams hoping that they can enter prestigious schools. Students are under much pressure to perform outstandingly on academic tests, and those who fail to do so can easily become social rejects in certain conservative-minded societies. Yet is it fair for students when the school curriculum is revolved around the building exam-taking skills? My stance on this is negative, and the reasons will be given in the following paragraph.

在亞洲地區的學校，總是花上許多時間來訓練學生如何考試，以期學生們能夠在全國入學考試中表現亮眼，進而進入聲譽良好的學校就讀，而學校這股耗費在學生考試技能上的精力，早已成為社會常態，但這般圍繞在升學考試上的課表，對學生來說真的是公平的嗎？對於這個問題，我的立場是反對的，且在下一段會一一列舉出反對的原因。

First and foremost, there have been countless examples of people who do not graduate from the top of school rankings, but are still tremendously successful in their choice of path. Take Jamie Oliver for example, the celebrity chef, who was early diagnosed with dyslexia, a disease preventing him from comprehending written words in a smooth manner, still manages to have all the success in the world in the competitive

industry of culinary craftsmanship. This goes to show that how individuals perform in school tests has no absolute connection with their success after graduation. Secondly, examinations are oftentimes only capable of testing individuals' certain areas of capabilities, such as one's short term memory. This type of test system isolates those who are endowed with other talents than doing exceptionally well on academic tests. They should also have the opportunity to be celebrated for their talents despite the fact that these talents might have nothing to do with taking a test.

　　首先，自古至今有許多並沒有畢業於所謂的明星學校，但在各界發展極為成功的人士們，舉傑米・奧利佛的例子來説，這位明星主廚在小時候被診斷出患有閱讀障礙，無法快速理解書面上的意思，但仍在競爭激烈的料理界闖出一片天，可見很多時候，考試的成績與畢業後的成就並沒有絕對的關連性；第二，考試的範圍，往往侷限於測試學生個體的背誦技能，而無法激發學生深入、全面性地去探討某學科範圍，而這種體制，孤立了不善考試，但卻擁有其它天賦的學生，但這些學生真不應該因為不善考試，而受到不平等對待。

Therefore, I do not think the education system is fair to all students, as it is not inclusive, but rather exclusive to those students who may have tremendous potential in other areas but test-taking. The intent behind the system is to find the best out of all students, but as we have come to understand, the best may not be found via this kind of search. It is like seeking a hare in a hen's nest, not the right way to go.

所以，我不認為現行的教育體系是公平的，主要是因為此體系不夠包容各種興趣、才能取向的學生，相反地，它對於不善考試的學生是非常不友善的，而原本以升學主義為導向的教育體系，其旨在於藉由考試、升學，來尋找天賦異稟的同學，但事實證明藉由此種體系來求才，可謂緣木求魚，是不妥善的。

1 教育

2 社會法律議題

3 民生生活

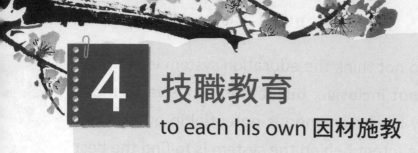

4 技職教育
to each his own 因材施教

成語閱讀故事

　　成語「因材施教」指的是老師依據學生各自的興趣、喜好及性格等個人特質，來設計不同的教學方式，以促使學生能夠快速地學習，並且更加有效率；其出處源自春秋時期，孔子的學生子路及冉有分別私下請教：「若聽到正確的主張時，是否應當立即行動？」，孔子建議子路在行動前先詢問兄長，但對冉有卻建議可直接施行，而孔子說明答案之所以會不同，就在於兩人的個性大不相同，子路較衝動，而冉有需更有自信；而在英文，有句話是用來形容每個人皆有屬於自己的偏好、個性，叫「to each his own」，與孔子「因材施教」背後的精神是一樣的。

寫作題目

Vocational schools provide education that equips students with practical skills. Such skills are expected to come in handy after graduation, especially when students enter the job market. In vocational schools, it is encouraged that students acquire knowledge through the design of hands-on curriculum and internship programs.

In Taiwan, 3-year vocational schools are in place as an alternative to senior high schools' general education. While senior high schools are traditionally held in high regard by society in general, the tide seems to be turning as students begin to choose vocational schools over general education, based on the belief that attaining trade-specific knowledge is a better use of 3 years than developing academic thinking and skills.

Do you agree with this emerging point of view, or not? Please explain.

寫作技巧解析

　　題目率先提到技職教育與一般高中教育的差別，並説明技職教育的重點放在專業技能的應用，而在現今社會中，技職教育受歡迎的程度已逐漸趕上傳統的普通高中，並且，許多人認為一般高中的課程並不實用，因其著重在各學科的學術培養上；以下範文採正面支持的立場，並且使用「to each his own」來形容每位學生的興趣及理想不盡相同，政府應藉由技職體系，落實孔子「因材施教」的教育理念。

應試撇步

　　在第一段裡，用「實際操作的 hands-on」這個形容詞來描述技職教育體系的課程，並説明有些學生已逐漸「感悟 come to the realization」到技職教育的優點；而在第二段，也解釋到有些學生天生「wired」、「長成、構成的」方式不同，各有較適合自己的學習方式，也如文章最後一句話提到的，每人「構成的 built」方式不同，因此教育也理當不同。

 作文範例

The line between general and vocational education has always been distinctive. Through general education, students are immersed in a variety of disciplines to develop a basic understanding of how the world operates, but mainly in the context of academic thinking. On the contrary, when it comes to vocational education, students are able to gain practical skills through hands-on practice. In recent years, vocational schools have been gaining more footing than in the past, as students start to come to the realization that spending time honing on applicable skills to work is worthier than spending delving into the scholarly piles of a certain discipline.

普通科教育與技職教育一直以來其界線、差別明顯,透過普教體系,學生專研於各學科,對於世界有了更深的認識,但主要還是侷限於學術上知識的成長,相反地,說到技職教育,學生得以藉由實作的練習,來學得畢業後能立即實際運用的技能;相比過去,技職學校在最近幾年越趨受歡迎,因學生已開始認為,學習能立即運用在工作職場上的技能,比花時間鑽研學術還要值得。

Along this line of thinking, I agree and believe that for a certain group of students, they should have the freedom to choose which kind of education they receive, and thus better off from that choice. The reason is that some students are wired to learn through physical experiences, the same as the fact that some students are born to comprehend faster through books and theories. For those students who will thrive in vocational schools, they should just avoid wasting time at traditional senior high schools, but should rather learn practical skills at a vocational school. The other reason lies in the gradual change of social perception where people do not hold academic achievements in as high a regard as in the past. Instead, vocational education is, in today's social climate, given the same weight as the traditional general education.

根據這個思維，我贊同某些特定的學生應有選擇自己受教育方式的權利，並因而發展得更好，因為有些學生天生適合藉由實際的經驗來學習，正如有些學生天生適合藉由書籍、理論來學習，而對於那些能夠在技職體系出類拔萃的學生們，理所當然地他們應該避免進入一般高中體系，以避免浪費時間在對於畢業後的工作無實質影響的事物上，另外，由於現在社會逐漸不像以前持有「唯有讀書高」的觀念，技職教育在現今的社會環境下，反而與一般高中體系一樣被重視。

In conclusion, given the arguments above, I fully support students' right to choose what kind of education would be best for them individually. After all, people are built differently to each his own, and they should be taught differently as well.

總結來說，綜合以上論述，我全力支持學生自由選擇適合自己教育的權利，因為人生而不同，而教育也應當因材施教，有所不同才是。

1 教育

2 社會法律議題

3 民生生活

5 補習

pay one's dues 急功近利

成語閱讀故事

「急功近利」這句成語，是用來形容某人過於看重名與利，而不擇手段、就只為了能夠盡快達到成功，且目光短淺，過度著眼於短期的利益，而忽略了長遠的考量，其出處來自漢・董仲舒《春秋繁露・對膠西王》中所提及的「仁人者正其道不謀其利，修其理不急其功。」，意謂有遠見的人，能夠平心靜氣、有所修為，而不會因短暫的利誘，而沉不住氣；在英文，會用「pay one's dues」來形容某人一步一腳印，認真努力以實踐成功，而其否定說法就可用來形容某人因為太專注於眼前所見，而無法瞭解真正重要的事物為何，與「急功近利」意思相仿。

In Asia, education system puts huge emphasis on how well students perform on each test.

This can be an ordinary test that students face in their own schools, or a national exam whose results will ultimately determine which school the exam-takers are attending.

Along with this phenomenon, cram schools are a common choice for students in search of ways to better prepare for exams, and in order to accommodate this demand, cram schools have shifted from focusing test-taking skills to the actual substance of knowledge in each subject.

Do you agree with this practice, or not? Please elaborate on your stance.

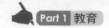

 寫作技巧解析

　　題目說到亞洲大部分的教育體系，較著重於學生考試的表現，不管是平常學校的小考，還是全國的升學考試，而也因為這樣，學生常常在下課後還去補習班，為的就是能夠在考試成績上取得領先，最終的結果就是補習班為了迎合此現象，將教學重點都放在各種考試技巧上，而不在於真正學問本質的領悟；以下範文採反對立場，並說明此種注重考試的「急功近利」的教學，使學生「do not want to pay their dues」，無法領悟到學科的精髓所在。

⊙ 應試撇步

　　在雅思的寫作考試中，最後一段應當簡單、明快地總結考生整篇文章的觀點及論述，所以在最後一段開頭的地方，可用如「in a nutshell」，或者是如「in short」、「in summary」、「in conclusion」等意為「簡單來說」、「整體來說」的片語，再接上考生簡短的文章總結；而考生應注意，最後一段的作用在於將整篇文章的重點加強，將整個論述濃縮到其最精華的部份，讓閱卷者能夠在讀完最後一段後，明確、鮮明地記住考生的觀點，及其列舉的支持論點為何，就會是個鏗鏘有力的作品。

 作文範例

 MP3 005

In most Asian countries, cram schools are viewed as a popular, efficient way for students to deal with the barrage of tests they face. Students are so bombarded with everyday tests that they are finally left with no choice but to seek guidance on how they can effectively perform well on piles of test papers everyday, a result of today's education system. The advent of cram schools, coupled with their development today, is the exact product of, if not the most appropriate testimony to, what our education system has become over the past couple of years. I take a stance against such test-driven approaches, especially those taken up by cram schools, and all the hype and buzz surrounding what those cram schools claim about in terms of training students to be better at taking tests.

在大部分的亞洲國家，補習班很受歡迎，且被視為輔助學生面對一連串考試的有效工具，而學生是如此地受到考試轟炸，他們被迫向補習班尋求協助，尋求如何有效地在這考試所築起的迷宮高牆中前進，而這無盡的考試正是現今教育體系的結果，另外，補習班的出現及其今日的發展，正是我們教育體系最近幾年走向的產物，甚可被形容為最具其代表性的象徵；我個人採反對立場，不認同這種以考試為取向教學方法，尤其是補習班如此以考試為重的教學，也不支持其誇大的行銷，聲稱能夠快速增進學生考試能力的效果。

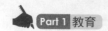

As of today, the disproportionate focus placed on test-taking skills of students, rather than a real understanding of subject matters at hand, is alarming. This kind of distorted approach to imparting knowledge is way off base, as students concentrate too much energy on how to acquire higher exam scores, but spend less energy on developing actual interest in each subject. In the short run, students might consider it beneficial for them to receive a helping hand with test-taking, which is warmly extended by cram school operators to assist with the masterful "art" of scoring excellent marks on tests. However, these perceived benefits can easily wear off once students pass the phase of exam-taking, and enter the stage of life where, inevitably, they are faced with a world where a true understating of a subject matter will be more importantly weighed upon than how well you can take a test in that subject matter.

直至今日，教育體系其極不均衡的著重在學生的考試能力，而不是著重在學生如何真正瞭解手邊的教學科目上，是讓人驚恐的。而這種扭曲的教學方式是偏離根本的，因其導致學生花費許多精力在學習如何於考試中取得高分，花費較少精力在瞭解各個學科背後的知識，而學生或許也會認為接受補習班的幫助，會是件獲益良多的事，尤其是在學習如何考試取得高分的「藝術」上，但這種認知上的獲益，很快就會被消磨掉，尤其當學生脫離考試的階段後，開始進入至人生另一個環節，學生們無法避免地將發現到，真正去瞭解一個學科的知識，將會比學習如何考試來的重要。

In a nutshell, the above-mentioned explanation sums up why I take a negative stance on how cram-schools operate today. In their efforts to help students excel on tests, they also push for the education system through which student do not pay their dues, as they become so wrapped up in the games of test-taking and do not care to develop genuine interest in the subjects which would be much more important in the long run.

簡短來説，上述的論點總結了我為何反對補習班現今營運的方式，因為當他們在努力教導學生如何考試的同時，他們也在協助倡導、推進這種教育體系，這種讓學生「短視近利」的教育體系，因為在這種教育體系下，學生不自覺地陷入考試的遊戲規則中，而沒有餘力來真正地瞭解、學習一個專科，但後者才是真正重要的，尤其當以長遠的眼光來看時。

6 資優班

Man is a product of his environment 一傅眾咻

📖 成語閱讀故事

　　「一傅眾咻」這句成語來自《孟子·滕文公下》，其中孟子對戴不勝說道：「若有人想要他的孩子學習齊國話，你認為他應該要請齊國人還是楚國人來教導他呢？」，戴不勝回應：「當然是應當請齊國人來教導如何說齊國話。」，但孟子接著解釋，就算是請齊國老師，但若孩子身處在楚國的環境，身邊的同伴都在耳邊不斷地以楚國話來干擾他，孩子還是無法成功地學習楚國話，因此，學習的環境對最終學習的成效是非常重要的；在英文中，有句話「Man is a product of his environment.」，也是相對形容環境及身邊的人，對於個人都有極大的影響。

寫作題目

In Asia, students with superior academic performance to their peers' are often granted the opportunity to enroll on what is called a "Gifted Class," where students have the chance to further develop and sharpen their skills in their naturally gifted areas of study than they possibly could in an average class.

By this division, students assigned to the "Gifted Class" are intensely trained, highly challenged, and competitively benchmarked against the rest of their equally qualified classmates to be the best version of themselves.

Do you agree with this division? Or do you think it is not appropriate to practice such division? Please explain your point of view.

寫作技巧解析

　　題目說道，在亞洲常有所謂的「資優班」的設置，為的就是能夠給予在某些學科上表現優異的學生，有更佳的機會及管道來發展他們在這些學科上的專業知識；以下範文將採正面的支持立場，用「Man is a product of his environment.」來解釋身邊環境的人事物，將會對個人學習的成效有極大的影響，而這些「資優班」的設置，以「一傅眾咻」的角度來看，將會對這些有天賦的學生帶來許多助益。

應試撇步

　　在第一段裡，有用到「*be endowed with*」這句片語，指的是某人有幸能夠擁有、或是承接極大的天賦、資產，而本篇的意思是指「資優班」的學生天資聰穎，「擁有極大的天賦」；另外，於最後一段用「*as the saying goes*」這句話，意思為「正如某句有名的話語所指的」，來帶出本篇的重點，也就是用該語「Man is a product of his environment.」這句話來形容環境對人影響的重要性。

 作文範例

MP3 006

In Asia, it is fairly common for schools to exclusively offer opportunities to those who showcase signs of huge potential in particular areas of study. These students are proffered a chance to enter what is commonly named "Gifted Class," whose aim is to maximally develop and sharpen both the intellect and skills of those who are massively endowed with explosive potential. My personal view is in alignment with such a practice, and will explain in the following paragraph.

在亞洲，學校常常會給予在某些科目展現獨特才能、才華的學生一些特別的機會，這些學生得以進入所謂的「資優班」，以利其盡其所能地來發展、磨練他們原本就極具潛能的技能或智商，我個人的觀點贊成這種「資優班」的制度，以下將詳述原因。

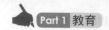

Generally speaking, the education system has the responsibility to ensure not only a level playing field for all parties involved, mainly the students, but also a place for those naturally gifted, especially those that are endowed with capabilities are bound to stand out more than their equal counterparts. In a situation where students considered top of the notch in certain areas of study are mixed with students that are not blessed in the same design, the former run the risk of being easily distracted. This will in turn deter those with ample aptitude from what they are able to achieve, and it would have been a different story only if these students in question were to learn in such an environment that is a match to the level of their intellectual charge. Thankfully, the "Gifted Class" provides the exact place that is homogenous, a place where students can expect to be educated and learn amongst people with similar aptitude and benchmarked the same.

通常來說，教育體制有義務來確保對所有的利益相關者，主要是學生，提供一個公平學習的環境，但也必須照顧到某些與同學齡相比，有才華、且能力出眾的學生盡情學習的平台，因他們的特殊才華，本身就注定會比同儕表現的還要亮眼；若這些在某些學科表現特別出眾的學生與普通學習能力的學生一起上課，前者可能會容易分心，進而影響到他們極力開發自己潛能的機會，但相反地，若是這些資質優異的學生與同等級的學生一起上課，將非常有可能會產生不同的結果，因此，幸好有「資優班」的誕生，提供了程度較好的學生在一個與自己實力相當、均質的環境學習的機會。

All in all, as the saying goes, "Man is a product of his environment," and this is exactly the spirit of what the "Gift Class" can do for those who, are blessedly ahead of the game than the rest of the population when it comes to certain subjects. Therefore, I agree with the practice of the "Gift Class."

總的來說，如成語「一傅眾咻」所指的，環境對於學習有極大的影響，而「資優班」所能做的，就是對那些在某些學科範圍內表現特別優異的學生，提供了足以激發其潛能的正面環境，因此，我贊同「資優班」的制度實施。

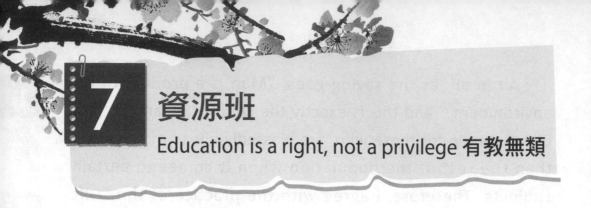

7 資源班
Education is a right, not a privilege 有教無類

📖 成語閱讀故事

　　「有教無類」是至聖先師孔子的另一句極為著名的話，他所指的是身為老師，應當對所有的學生一視同仁，不應該因為學生本身如社會地位等外在因素，而在教學方面上有所不同的待遇，而如此進步的理念，可謂今日廣泛實施的平民教育之先河；在英文中，經常聽到「Education is a right, not a privilege.」這句話，其背後的精神，也就是「有教無類」所倡導的，認為受教育對任何人來說，都是本身應有的權利，而不是一種特權。

In school, there is the so-called "Resource Room' designated for students who are in need of special attention, or with some type of learning disabilities, to receive education.

Without a doubt, the creation and design of "Resource Room" is out of goodwill, making sure students who are with special needs can receive education. In a "Resource Room" class, teaching materials are specifically designed to meet the students' learning curve, and hopefully be instrumental in their achieving of best potential.

However, there has been certain attached stigma, in some cases even discrimination, when it comes to societies' view of the "Resource Room." What is your take on this? Please explain.

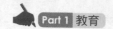

寫作技巧解析

　　題目說到在許多學校，有所謂「資源班」的設立，目的是讓有需要特別關注、或是有學習障礙的孩子能夠得到適合的教育，然而，儘管「資源班」最初設立的立意，是以最能幫助這些需要特別教育的孩子而所設想的，社會上偶爾還是有人會對於「資源班」持著負面觀感；以下範文採取支持、正面立場，並引用「有教無類 Education is a right, not a privilege.」這句話來支持論述。

應試撇步

　　本文在第二段一開頭即開宗明義地指出「有教無類 *Education is a right, not a privilege.*」，並說明有學習障礙的孩子不應該「被懲罰 *punished*」，「更不用說 *let alone*」被剝奪教育的權益了，並說明教育對於有學習障礙的孩子是極其重要的，而我們身為社會的一份子，應當以更加「包容 *inclusive*」的態度來面對他們的學習才是。

作文範例

The set-up of "Resource Room" in school is intended to support the providence of proper education to those who are in need of a different kind of education approach. Without question, the intention behind such designated resources towards giving and instilling survival skills in those who have a hard time taking care of themselves is benevolent. However, it is inevitable for certain people in societies to attach stigma to those being educated in a "Resource Room." I oppose such a twisted view on something being done out of goodwill, and will explain in the following paragraph.

「資源班」的設立是為了提供給需要不同教育管道的學生合適的教育，無庸置疑地，如此特別的資源配置，提供給連照顧自己都有困難的學生學習存活的教育，此背後的立意是良善的，但是，無可避免地，社會中的某些人會將在「資源班」學習的孩子汙名化，而我反對這種扭曲的態度，尤其當它是對於此種利益良善的機制，並將於下段詳細論述。

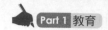

First of all, as the saying goes, "Education is a right, not a privilege." Those who are born with learning disabilities should not be punished, let alone to be stripped of their right to education. As it would not be a conducive and nurturing environment for them to go through learning at a conventional classroom setting, the least government can do is to provide a healthy, appropriate alternative for them. Secondly, education is an especially serious matter to those with learning disabilities, as without education, they might not be able to even sustain or maintain their basic life needs. That is why we, the society as an agglomerate of humanity, should be more inclusive towards those who study in a "Resource Room."

首先，如俗話所說的，「有教無類」，若天生有學習困難的孩子，不應該被處罰，更不應該被剝奪教育的權利，而因為一般的傳統教室學習環境，對他們來說並不是有助益、滋養的環境，所以政府至少應提供給這些孩子一個健康的、適宜的替代方案；第二點，教育對於這些孩子來說是個嚴肅的議題，因為若沒有適當的教育，他們或許連照顧自身基本的需求都有問題，這就是為什麼我們身為社會大家庭的一份子，應對於這些「資源班」的孩子更加包容才是。

In summary, people are born equal, and no matter their race, social rank, country, or whichever factor that is considered at play when it comes to our being, we should always have the right to education. There should definitely be no stigma attached to people learning, no matter in which shape or form, but rather the learning itself should always be fostered, promoted, and encouraged.

總結來說，人生而平等，不論種族、社會階級、國家或是任何被視為會影響自身的各種因素，皆不能影響我們受教育的權利，也不應該有任何形式的汙名與學習做連結，反之，應當持續培育、倡導及鼓勵任何形式的教育。

8 批判性思考

jump on the bandwagon 讀書不知味，不如束高閣

成語閱讀故事

　　「讀書不知味，不如束高閣」，其源來自清代詩人袁枚所創作的一首有關讀書主題的詩，其用意在於警示後代的讀書人，在用功苦讀、鑽研學術之餘，別忽略了批判性思考、理解的重要性，要不然只是純粹性地苦讀，而沒有自己的獨立思考去判斷、過濾所吸收的學識的話，還「不如束高閣」，還不如將這些書冊捆起來好好存放；在英文，若要形容某人不深思熟慮，只跟著大眾的潮流、思想走，可用「jump on the bandwagon」來形容這種行為，就如「讀書不知味，不如束高閣」一樣，在形容沒有獨自思考批判的行為。

Today, people hold different views to what the ultimate goal of education should be. Generally speaking, in a western educational system, focus has been much put upon the developing of individual critical thinking among students. On the contrary, the Asian educational systems do not put as much weight on such a development as their western counterparts do.

The Asian educational systems have been traditionally focused more on rote learning. Students in Asia are expected to absorb knowledge in a limited timeframe and are asked to regurgitate what they have learned exactly as what they are taught.

Do you agree with the western focus or the Asia one?

1 教育

2 社會法律議題

3 民生生活

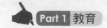
寫作技巧解析

以下範文將採取贊同西式教育的態度，並且解釋若沒有獨立批判性思考的能力，學生在畢業進入社會後，將會有一段適應期，因為在現實社會中，很多事情是沒有所謂的對與錯，端看個人怎麼去思考、詮釋手邊的資訊，再依照個人所思考的結果，去做一個最好的決定，因此，學校必須注意別讓學生「讀書不知味，不如束高閣」，別讓學生養成「jump on the bandwagon」的習慣才好。

應試撇步

在第二段中，有使用到「follow in someone's footsteps」這句動詞片語，來解釋在現實生活中，並沒有一定的規範、準則來讓人們追隨、參考；之後也說道，畢業後的人生，不像學校考試的「多選題」，有一定的選項可以參考，而「多選題」的英文是「multiple choice questions」，而在最後一段總結時也說道，若學校只能教育出「jump on the bandwagon」的學生的話，那真是「讀書不知味，不如束高閣」，是沒有意義的。

 作文範例　　　　　　　　　 MP3 008

In the western educational system, schools focus their resources and energy on developing students' critical thinking abilities. In contrast, in an Asian educational system, students are more expected to learn in a subservient way, meaning it is not highly encouraged for students to form an opinion of their own, especially such an opinion that challenges the authority of education providers. My personal view is that students should be more exposed to learning materials and programs that ignite critical thinking, and below explains why.

在西方的教育體系，學校將資源及精力著重在發展學生的批判性思考能力，相反地，在亞洲的教育體系，對於學生的期望是希望學生能夠乖巧、好學，並不鼓勵學生有太多自己獨特的想法，尤其是對於挑戰老師權威的想法及意見，而我個人認為學生應當處在能夠激發個人批判性思考的教學，以下詳述原因。

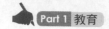

For starters, the ultimate goal for education should be to better prepare students for the real world so that they are bound to enter at some point in their lives. In real life, people need to make decisions based on critical thinking, as there is rarely a firm set of guidelines that tell people which path is the correct one to embark on, or which footsteps are the right ones to follow in, especially in relation to dealing with something as complicated in nature as life is. Life after graduation is not as simple as taking a test, where spaces are to be filled with multiple choices; it requires extensive thinking, and it requires people to make a series of decisions based off of their judgment on the general situation, the nuances that differ in each situation, and to critically evaluate each outcome that comes along with each decision made.

首先，教育的最終目標，應該是幫助學生能夠做好未來進入社會的準備，而在現實生活中，人們必須靠批判性思考來做許多決定，因為其實並沒有真正的一套準則來告訴大家人生中正確的道路怎麼走，尤其畢業後的現實人生是很複雜的，並不像在學校考試一樣，有一定的選項可以選擇，現實人生需要廣泛地思考，並需要依據各種狀況來做不同的判斷，並批判性地來評斷各種決定可能會造成的結果才行。

When put this way, there is no difficulty seeing how critical thinking plays a huge role in modern society, and students are supposed to be better trained in that regard. There is really no point for education when what all students learn in school is how to jump on the bandwagon of someone else's opinions, and that is why I agree with the Western approach to education.

這樣說來，讀者應不難看出批判性思考在現今社會的重要性，因為若教育系統只能教育出無法自己思索、判斷的學生的話，正如「讀書不知味，不如束高閣」所形容的，盲目地跟隨身邊的意見，這樣是行不通的，所以我較贊成西式的教育方針。

1 教育

2 社會法律議題

3 民生生活

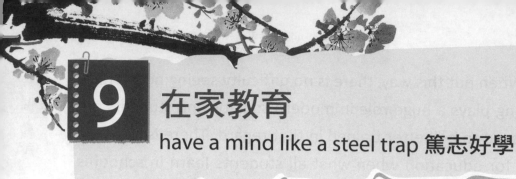

9 在家教育

have a mind like a steel trap 篤志好學

　　成語「篤志好學」是用來形容某人樂於學習，且意志堅定，樂於在自己所喜好的學習科目上，更加鑽研、精進，以求更上一層樓；在英文裡，有句諺語可用來形容某人天資聰穎，能夠快速地學習新的事物，這句諺語是「have a mind like a steel trap」，「steel trap」是古代獵捕動物的器具，當野獸一不小心踩在這個器具上時，「steel trap」能夠快速地反應，夾住野獸的腳掌，因此當用這個器具來形容一個人的學習能力時，也就是正面的讚賞某人學習具有熱情、快速，正如「篤志好學」所形容的意思。

In some parts of the world, parents have the liberty of choosing what they feel is in their children's best interests to send them to school for learning. If not, they have the alternative to choose homeschooling, formally known as home education, for their children.

There are obviously pros and cons to each method, and there certainly has been much heated discussions surrounding this issue. Some people believe homeschooled children are at a huge disadvantage while others disagree.

What is your take on this? Which of these two educational methods do you think is best suited for children's needs of learning? Please provide supporting arguments for your stance.

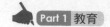

寫作技巧解析

　　以下範文將採取支持學校教育的立場，而反對在家教育，其原因在於學校教育能夠提供學生學習如何與其它人相處的機會，而在家教育則無法；內文提到，不論孩子是多麼地「篤志好學」，是多麼地「have a mind like a steel trap」，社交技巧還是需要實際操作、學習的，若沒有提供他們這個機會，將來在現實社會中，與各式各樣的人相處時，無可避免地還是會需要一段適應期。

應試撇步

　　在第二段中，有用到單字「microcosm」來形容學校為社會的「縮影」，是個好用且較為進階的名詞單字，適合用在各種主題；另外，所謂的「社交技巧」，英文叫作「interpersonal skills」，也就是人與人之間相處、溝通的技巧，而之所以稱為「技巧」，而不是稱為「知識」，就是因為「技巧」必須「做中學 from actual doing」，不像「知識」可以純粹藉由閱讀取得。

 作文範例　　　　　　　　　　　　　🔘 MP3 009

In certain parts of the world, parents are faced with the dilemma of whether their country's educational system is suited enough for their children. In other words, do they have enough confidence in the educational system to put their children's learning, especially at a stage of life where they are the most impressionable and moldable by surrounding influences, in the hands of the system? Some parents eventually opt for homeschooling over school, and decide to take ownership of their children's education. I disagree with such practice, and would argue that education at school comes with advantages that are irreplaceable by other forms of education, such as homeschooling.

在這世界的某些區域，家長面臨了決定其所處的國家教育體制是否適合他們家孩子的難題，換句話說，家長必須考慮是否有足夠的信心將他們的孩子交給國家的教育體系，而這並不是一件簡單的事，因為孩子的教育，尤其還小的時候，對於人格的養成是很有影響的；有些家長最終選擇將孩子留在家裡自學，而不選擇學校教育，將孩子教育的義務往自己身上承攬，而我並不認同在家教育的實施，因為學校教育有一些優勢，是無法被其它教育方式所取代的，包括在家教育。

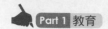

One of the advantages for education at school is to have the opportunity presented to students to interact and mingle with all kinds of personalities. Schools may be considered a microcosm of the real world, where interpersonal skills are an integral part of everyday life. Homeschooling strips children of such opportunities. No matter how much these children have a mind like a steel trap, they all need to experience interpersonal relationships firsthand to figure out and learn how to make friends with others and how they are going to fit in a group setting. As it is called "interpersonal skills," students need to learn from their actual experiences of interacting with others.

學校教育其中的一個優點，就是讓學生有與各種個性的同學互動、交流的機會，而學校可說是現實社會的縮影，在現實社會中，與人互動的技巧是非常重要的，而自學教育剝奪了孩子學習此項技能的機會，不論這些孩子是多麼地篤志好學，他們都需要親身去體驗怎麼交朋友，如何在團體中生活等等，而之所以會稱為社交「技能」，指的就是必須做中學，不是僅僅藉由閱讀就可以學會的。

In short, from the above-discussed aspect, social abilities are one key element of education for children. When educated purely at home, students miss out on the opportunities of learning how to make friends, how to handle themselves in situations when having friction with others, and how to take other's feelings into consideration, to name but a few. On the other hand, this can be greatly learned at school, and will be a great asset for the students in the rest of their lives.

簡單來說，以上所敘述的項目，是教育的一個重要環節，若學生只是純粹在家學習的話，將失去交朋友、學習協調不同意見，及學習擁有同理心等機會，但相反地，他們可在學校好好學習這些技能，而餘生也將受益於這些技能的取得。

1 教育

2 社會法律議題

3 民生生活

10 胎教

if you lie down with dogs, you will get up with fleas 芝蘭之室

成語閱讀故事

　　成語「芝蘭之室」，其源由來自孔子所說的：「與善人居，如入芝蘭之室，久而不聞其香，即與之化矣。」形容的即是環境對人潛移默化的影響力，藉由進入到一個充滿花香的房間，來形容與好的人在一起，一開始會有如聞到花香一般，他的優點、長處會很突出、引人注意，但久了之後，就有如花香般，漸漸不會被注意到，因為你默默的也被他同化了，所以自然不會再覺得稀奇；在英文裡，有句類似的諺語，不過是以負面的觀點來陳述同樣的事情，叫作「if you lie down with dogs, you will get up with fleas」，指的也是環境對人的重要性，以及久了之後會被同化的現象。

 寫作題目

People have always been learning for their whole lives, and studies have shown that people who are still working at older ages would have both a better mental and physical health than their counterparts.

However, it may come as a surprise that nowadays, we as human beings are expected to learn before we are even born. The term "Prenatal Education" is all the rage now, claiming that there are certain activities that parents can do with their children during pregnancy.

There is no thorough scientific proof yet in relation to such claims, but in your personal views, do you agree with the concept? Please explain.

1 教育

2 社會法律議題

3 民生生活

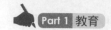
寫作技巧解析

　　以下範文將採取正面支持的態度，說明胎教的重要性，並且以環境影響人性的觀點來切入，並以諺語「if you lie down with dogs, you will get up with flees」來加強説明不論在人生的哪一個階段，就算還在媽媽的肚子裡，都免不了會受到身邊的環境影響，並列舉一些胎教的方法，來增加文章的趣味性。

應試撇步

　　若要形容孩子尚未生出、還在懷孕階段，可用「during pregnancy」來形容，另外，「prenatal」這個形容詞是用來形容在孩子正式生出前所發生的事，所以「胎教」的正式英文為「Prenatal Education」，也就是孩子出生之前所受到有關教育的活動，而文章最後也有提到普遍的「胎教」，包含了讓肚子中的孩子聽古典音樂「listen to classical music」，或是賞析藝術作品「appreciate pieces of art」等等。

 作文範例　　　　　　　　　　　　　　🔘 MP3 010

　　Starting education to kids while they are in moms' bellies is very popular among soon-to-be parents in today's society. Although science has not provided proof to support what is called "Prenatal Education," people are certainly more than willing to try all means to give their babies a head start as early as the time during pregnancy. My personal view on this is that it is very possible what parents do during pregnancy would have a certain impact on how children turn out, and people should be mindful of that.

　　在現今的社會中，準父母很流行在孩子還在媽媽肚子裡的時候，就開始孩子的教育，儘管科學尚未證實所謂的「胎教」的影響，人們還是很樂在其中，藉由各種有趣的方法，來盡全力地將孩子塑造成最好的樣子，而我個人的觀點是認為「胎教」是非常有可能會對孩子有著一定程度的影響，所以大家都應該多注意這方面的事情。

Throughout all stages of human life, there is no denying that the environment around us would have a huge impact on what kind of person we turn out to be. As the saying goes, "When you lie down with dogs, you will get up with fleas." This old adage reinforces the idea that outer influences, whether positive or negative, all have their individual effects on us. Human beings are used to picking up habits when they are exposed to certain kinds of behavior long enough. So why would it be any different for them in the prenatal stage, one of the most impressionable stages of human beings as we are still forming and developing during pregnancy. Some interesting ways to "Prenatal Education" are to play classical music to mothers' bellies, or ask mothers to regularly browse through art pieces and beautiful pictures, and so on.

在人生的各個階段中，身旁的環境，當接觸一定的時間後，對我們的言行舉止有很大的影響是不可否認的，也就是成語「芝蘭之室」所描述的情形，這句成語加強了有關外在環境對我們影響的論述，不論那外在環境是正面還是負面的，而在剛接觸新環境的時候，我們理所當然會對身邊某些人事物的特質非常敏感，但時間久了之後，我們也將對這些特質漸漸習慣、麻木，而尚未出生的胎兒何嘗不是如此呢？尤其胎兒是處在人生中最易受影響的階段之一，因為他們還在生長、成形中，而有關「胎教」的一些有趣的方法，包括了對著媽媽的肚子播放古典音樂，或是媽媽經常、規律性地瀏覽藝術作品、美麗的照片等等。

Shortly speaking, I am in full support of "Prenatal Education." Parents should do everything they can to further the development of their children, even when it means to do so during pregnancy, not to mention that parents would also have fun while listening to classical music and appreciating pieces of art.

簡短來說，我很支持「胎教」的作法，因為家長應當盡全力來幫助孩子成長，而在孩子出生前的懷孕期間就應該開始實行，更何況在實施「胎教」的過程中，家長也可以一起享受聆聽古典音樂，一起賞析藝術作品。

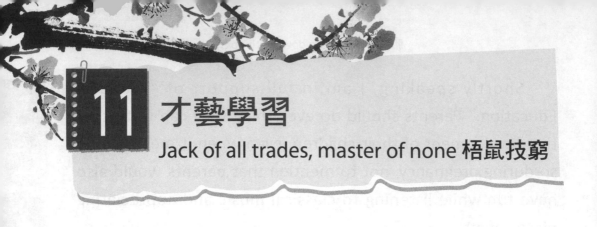

11 才藝學習
Jack of all trades, master of none 梧鼠技窮

📖 成語閱讀故事

　　成語「梧鼠技窮」的出處來自《荀子・勸學》中所説的「騰蛇無足而飛，梧鼠五技而窮。」，意思是指在某一項技能的專精，遠比在各個領域都學，但卻都學而不精還要好，而荀子話中所提到的「騰蛇」，指的是某一種龍，形容牠雖沒有腳，卻能因專精而翱遊天際，反觀「梧鼠」雖有五項技能，但卻樣樣不精、才能有限，最終也只能侷限在地上活動；在英文裡，可用諺語「Jack of all trades, master of none」來形容此種情況，其指的就是某人對於各項技能都去學習、嘗試，但卻因學習太多事物，而無法花足夠的時間來真正地成為某項技能的專家。

寫作題目

Nowadays, many parents put much pressure on their children to master all sorts of talents. The most popular ones include the mastering of skills, such as playing the piano, strumming the guitar, hitting high notes while singing, etc.

If there is an area of interest in the marketplace, whether academic or extracurricular, there will definitely be a cram school offering classes for it.

Although parents are well-intended for pushing children to acquire as many talents as possible, many question the efficacy of such an intensive training.

What is your viewpoint on this phenomenon? Are you in support of this, or not? Please explain.

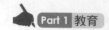

寫作技巧解析

　　以下範文採取反對的立場，認為家長若要求孩子學習過多的才藝，孩子極有可能會因為一次學習太多而吃不消，終將導致孩子無法專精於任何一項才藝，反而是得不償失的；為了加強論點，文章在第二段一開頭就用諺語「Jack of all trades, master of none」來引出現代孩子的窘境，並接著再以例子來輔助說明。

應試撇步

　　文章第二段中用形容詞「負擔過重的 *overburdened*」這個單字來形容因過多才藝課程而「渾身乏術 *spread too thin*」的學子，並用「*dabble in*」這個動詞片語來指出，被迫學習各種才藝的孩子，最終也只能「涉獵、淺學」這些所學的才藝，而無法在任一個項目「專精、成為專家 *become an expert of*」，並指出若能給孩子們「多點體諒 *cut some slack*」，反而對家長及孩子是較有助益的。

作文範例

MP3 011

In the current state of the society in general, parents want nothing more than developing their children in every capacity. Parents encourage children to explore as many talents as possible, especially in the golden age of childhood, which is supposed to be the most efficient time to learn in the entirety of human life, and acquire the skills of new things. However, I am not in support of this kind of mentality, and will explain why in the following paragraph.

以目前的社會概況來說，家長們總是希望能夠盡量發展孩子的潛能，因此經常鼓勵孩子多元發展，尤其趁孩子還處在人生的黃金歲月時，把握此時人生中最易吸收、學習新知的時光，讓孩子多方面地來學習各式各樣的才藝，然而我並不完全認同此心態，並會在下一段解釋原因。

As the saying goes, "Jack of all trades, master of none." This saying perfectly embodies the sentiment behind overburdened students who have been spread too thin. Besides, the balance between the number of talent classes that children need to attend and the free time reserved for them to just be children is often hard to define. Unfortunately, children are found to be overloaded with way too many courses. Children have to attend sports classes, learn how to play musical instruments, develop artistic interests through craftsmanship workshops, and the list goes on. As a result, children have no choice but to be dabbling in, rather than to become an expert of everything that they are forced to come in contact with. This outcome is certainly not desired by both parents and children, and it would be much more beneficial for parents to cut their children some slack.

正如成語「梧鼠技窮」所形容的，其也完美詮釋出負荷過重、繁忙學生們的心聲，此外，孩子們課外才藝班的課程安排，以及孩子們所能享有的自由時間、能夠盡情地玩耍，其中的平衡是很難拿捏的，然而不幸地，家長總是給孩子太多負荷，要求他們參加過多的才藝班，如運動、樂器演奏、手工藝等課程，而結果就是學生們在各個他們被逼迫學習的領域中淺度學習、接觸，但都不是很專精，而這個結果必定不是大家所樂見的，還不如給孩子們多一點喘息的空間，是比較有幫助的。

In short, I do not agree with the practice of bombarding children with a myriad of talent classes. It is no point in learning so many things on the surface level, but being proficient at none.

簡短來說，我並不贊同以過多的才藝班來轟炸、逼迫孩子們學習的方式，因為若最終的結果都只是淺學、什麼都不精通的話，是毫無意義的。

12 語言學習
connect the dots 觸類旁通

📖 成語閱讀故事

　　成語「觸類旁通」是用來形容某人藉由學習、接觸某一方面的知識，而能夠進一步延伸，以將所學的知識及概念應用到其它類似的領域上，其出處來自《周易‧系辭上》所提到的「引而伸之，觸類而長之，天下之能事畢矣。」，所提倡的即是能夠舉一反三，將所學融會貫通至其它相關領域的學習方法；在英文的使用上，可用「connect the dots」來形容某人將事情融會貫通的動作，其意思與成語「觸類旁通」相近，都是指某人能夠藉由單一領域、事件的學習，而將其所學沿用、引伸到其它類似的事物上。

1 教育

2 社會法律議題

3 民生生活

Learning a second language is often an arduous process, especially when that language is totally different from a person's native language.

However, as many languages as there are in the world, certain languages can be grouped together as they may have the same origins or just evolved into variants over time. Then they may have surprising similarities through either trade or colonization during a certain period of time in history.

On the other hand, even in a single language, some ways of expression can be better conveyed though the structure of one particular language than others.

With this conflicting nature of language learning in mind, do you think it is a good idea for educators to apply "learning by association" techniques while teaching languages? Please explain.

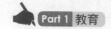

寫作技巧解析

　　題目首先提到第二語言的學習經常不是個輕鬆的過程，尤其當所學習的第二語言與某人的母語差異甚大時，會更加地困難，而這也帶出了在世界上的眾多語言中，有某些語言因來自同一體系，所以有許多的相似之處，但每個語言也都有其獨特之處，因此題目詢問考生是否認為「關聯性學習法」適用在語言學習的範疇上；以下範文採取支持的立場，並認為學習語言應當盡量「connect the dots」，以「觸類旁通」的方式來學習，事半功倍。

應試撇步

　　第一段中提到的片語「have something in common」指的是某些事物有什麼共通點，可用來替換單字「相似、共同點 similarities」，以增加文章的變化；第二段所使用的片語「on each end of the spectrum」，字面上的意思為「在光譜的兩端」，所指的即是兩者差異甚大，之後用「在什麼方面 in terms of」搭配「地理 geography」來敘述儘管英文與日文在地球的兩端，但在日文中有許多的外來語皆與英文的很多單字有共通、相似之處。

 作文範例　　　🎧 MP3 012

Languages around the world are surely very different, especially when you look and compare them from different regions. However, languages from the same origins do instead have many similarities than expected. Based on this fact, I strongly encourage the use of "learning by association" techniques while teaching languages that possess words, grammar, ways of thinking, and other aspects of things in common.

全世界的語言是非常不同的，尤其是來自不同區域的語言，但是同一區域中的語言的確有許多非預期的相同之處，而正因如此，我強烈支持在教導具有相同字詞、文法、邏輯及其它共通之處的語言時，使用「關聯性學習法」的技巧來教學。

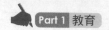

First of all, "learning by association" describes the teaching methodology where students are encouraged to apply what they have learned to other areas of study. In other words, pupils are taught and trained to connect the dots of various disciplines so that they are flexible enough to absorb knowledge in a much more efficient way. As in the arena of language learning, one example can be found in the language of Japanese, whose words share the same roots with the English language, despite the fact that Japan and other English-speaking countries are geographically far apart. This phenomenon can be explained by human history and the involvement of international trade, and learners of language today ought to utilize such convenience to their best advantage in order to learn world languages in a much more productive way.

首先，「關聯性學習法」指的是鼓勵學生將某一方面的所學應用、延伸至其它可應用的範圍的教學方法，換句話說，學生被教導、訓練以觸類旁通的方式，來更有效率地學習，而在語言學習的競技場中，日文就是個很好的例子，雖然它與英文可謂發源於地球上的兩個極端，但因歷史及貿易的發展，它們享有許多相似的字詞，而今日的語言學習者應當善加利用此方便性，來更加有效率地學習世界各種語言。

All in all, I support the use of "leaning by association" methodology to boost the efficacy of language learning. One thing to keep in mind is that language learning is an organic and ever-evolving process, which can be made effortlessly if the habit of connecting the dots is applied.

總結來説，我支持「關聯性學習法」的教學使用，來幫助語言學習的成效，而我們應謹記語言學習是個有機、不斷變化的過程，若能習慣以觸類旁通的方式來學習，在學習上會是不費吹灰之力的。

13 公職考試

Diamonds are made under pressure 生於憂患，死於安樂

成語閱讀故事

　　成語「生於憂患，死於安樂」所形容的是有憂患意識的人，將會更加努力、勤奮地工作，而相反的，若沒有憂患意識，而只在乎享樂的人，將會因未察覺出相關潛在的危險，因而過於安逸，但也將導致自身的毀滅；在英文中，經常會聽到「Diamonds are made under pressure.」這句話，其字面意思為「鑽石在高壓下生成」，形容的即是「生於憂患，死於安樂」這個成語所勸告的，若生活過於安逸、沒有外在壓力，將很有可能導致自己的失敗，而無法如鑽石般在歷經高壓後光芒閃耀。

In Taiwan, the society oftentimes views the profession of public servants in a negative light. This is mainly because the profession is perceived as such a secure job that many believe these jobholders are not properly kept on their toes to ensure an efficient running of public affairs.

However, despite such an unflattering attitude towards the profession, many youngsters are still much interested in taking the national exam, vying for the few positions that are released each year.

As intense as the national exam could be, given the large number of applicants but only a few fixed openings, those successful applicants find themselves not incentivized to achieve more after taking office.

What is your view on this? Please state your rationale behind your view.

寫作技巧解析

　　題目提到，台灣社會有時對於公務員抱持著負面的觀感，主要是因為公務員的工作被認為是鐵飯碗，而也因為這樣，許多人認為公務員不用戰戰兢兢、有隨時被解雇的壓力，儘管公職考試競爭激烈，社會普遍觀感認為公務員在考完試、就職後，因沒有足夠的激勵、壓力，而怠惰，進而影響公務效率；以下範文認為應當改革公務員考核機制，創造適當壓力，因為「生於憂患，死於安樂 Diamonds are made under pressure.」，唯有如此，全民的福祉才更能把握、增進。

應試撇步

　　範文提到，公務人員的職業，對於大學畢業生來說，是個具有「誘惑、誘因 allure」的職業，因為公務員被視為是個鐵飯碗，但由於缺乏適當的獎懲制度，「用人唯才 meritocracy」的措施難以「實施 implement」，再加上公務員的工作本身與政治有著緊密的關係，也因此「裙帶關係 nepotism」難以完全杜絕，所以範文認為，要改善公務人員效率的第一步，應當「根本改革、翻修 overhaul」現行的工作評鑑制度，以激勵公務員在工作上爭取好的表現。

 作文範例

MP3 013

In the Taiwanese society, the profession of public servants is an ideal occupation for fresh college graduates. The allure of such a profession partially comes from its perceived status of being a secure job position for life. However, with that perceived security, public servants are also often criticized for being too lax in their dealings with public affairs as no proper amount of pressure is placed on them. Granted, these jobholders are ought to be of great quality as they are those who have come out on top out of tens of thousands of applicants vying for those coveted spots. Therefore, the government should really take into serious consideration as to how to properly harness such potentially powerful reserves of workforce that, if properly prodded and managed, could have a huge impact on the development of the island country.

在台灣的社會中，公務員職位是大學畢業生嚮往、理想的工作，而公務員職位部分令人嚮往的誘因，來自於其終身鐵飯碗的觀感。然而，也因為這安全的觀感，公務員有時會被批評他們對於公務的處理過於怠惰，因為他們並沒有感到足夠的壓力。當然，這些公務員理當為高素質人員，因為他們能夠在萬人遴選考試中脫穎而出。所以，政府應當仔細、認真思考該如何駕馭底下的公務人員，要是能夠適當管控、激勵這些擁有強大潛力的公務人力資源，其對台灣島國的發展，將具有舉足輕重的影響。

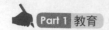

For years, the governmental ways to conduct performance reviews on public servants have been much criticized by critics as not being transparent, not based on meritocracy, and not holding the reviewers accountable for their given-out performance audits. Also, as closely involved as public servants are with their inner workings with politics, nepotism is not easy to completely rid of, making the practice of meritocracy much harder to implement. Hence, I propose the first step to improve public servant's work efficiency is to overhaul the current performance review methods to a more transparent, merit-based one.

多年來，政府對於底下公務員所施行的工作表現評鑑的方法，備受爭議，許多評論家認為這些評鑑方法不夠透明，不是純粹由個人的工作表現來評鑑，且評鑑者還不需為自己所給予的評鑑負責。另外，公務員本身的工作範圍、權責，與政治幕後的操作很密切，也因此裙帶關係難以杜絕，所以任人唯才的施政難以落實；因此，我主張改善公務員效率的第一步，就是政府應當根本地改革目前所實施的工作評鑑方針，改為透明、用人唯才的評鑑方法。

As diamonds are made under pressure, public servants will increase efficiency if they are properly pressured and incentivized. Besides, if public servants are subject to a fairer method of performance audit, they would be more inclined to strive for a better work performance as well.

正如生於憂患，死於安樂所述，公務員在適當的獎懲壓力下，才會提升工作效率，並且，他們在較公平的工作評鑑制度下，也才更有可能自發上進，在工作表現上努力。

1 教育

2 社會法律議題

3 民生生活

14 廣設大學
a drop in the ocean 車載斗量

　　成語「車載斗量」是用來形容某一個事物的數量非常龐大，其出處來自《三國志》中吳國的趙咨所言：「如臣之比，車載斗量，不可勝數。」，當時趙咨是在回應魏國主公曹丕所提的問題，詢問吳國有多少位如趙咨般有才華的人才，而趙咨就以這段話來回應，敘述吳國如他有才華般的人才多到數不清，就算用再多的車來載送、或用再多的斗桶來測量，都還是無法勝數的；而在英文中，常形容某個事物有如「a drop in the ocean」一般，來指與其類似的事物極多，而它這個事物本身的存在就有如大海中的一滴水，並不是特別稀奇的。

 寫作題目

In Taiwan, there are currently a great number of established colleges and universities. On the contrary, there has been a consistent decline in birth rates in Taiwan.

As these factors go into play, the market of Taiwan's higher education is very well likely to be thrown out of balance, and can bring great ramifications if not carefully dealt.

On the other hand, some trumpet the idea of having colleges and universities in abundance, and may consequently much reduce the stress that come with students taking national entrance exams for higher education. What is your take on this? Please explain.

1 教育

2 社會法律議題

3 民生生活

寫作技巧解析

題目說道台灣的教育體系發展至今，造成了今日廣設大學的現象，雖然造成此現象的最初立意是為了讓考大學的學生們壓力能夠減輕，但近年來台灣少子化的現象持續，並未有好轉的跡象，在未來將會有供過於求的問題產生；以下範文認為台灣大學的林立並不是好的現象，並認為大學的設立已如同「a drop in the ocean」，沒有太大的意義，因為在台灣大學已是「車載斗量」，並不稀奇了。

應試撇步

本篇範文運用到「供需法則 supply and demand」的概念來解釋台灣現今廣設大學的現象，並在第一段用「omnipresence」這個名詞來說明大學目前「無處不在」的現象，且也在最後一段，用形容詞「ubiquitous」來形容同樣的現象，最後提到政府應思考相對應的大學「退場」機制，用動詞片語「phase out」來說明「逐步淘汰」的對應措施。

1 教育

2 社會法律議題

3 民生生活

In Taiwan, there is such a great number of colleges and universities that are currently established for students to enroll. However, Taiwan has seen a decline in birth rates over the last couple of years. Although the omnipresence of today's colleges and universities can be traced back to the goodwill of certain groups to alleviate pupils' stress level, the abundant supply has posed quite a few problems on the Taiwanese society and economy. Therefore, I oppose such widespread set-up of a myriad of colleges and universities.

台灣的教育體系演化至今，已演變成有太多的大學可供選擇，然而台灣近年來生育率卻持續下滑。儘管現今大學無處不在的現象始於讓應屆考試學生壓力減輕的好意，這過多的大學供給將會造成社會及經濟上的問題，因此，我並不贊同如此普遍的大學設立。

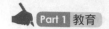

For starters, as the birth rates in Taiwan have been declining, and show no sign of pace in any foreseeable future, there will soon be a shortage of students. This is a real threat to many of those redundant colleges and universities as it is no secret that the running of educational institutions is very much alike the running of business conglomerates as they both indeed need monetary resources in order to last for long. Hence, the incoming shortage of students means that a shortage of tuition fees, and college and universities have no choice but to close down. Moreover, the abundance of higher educational institutions will lead to an overly easy access for students who will probably not need to work as hard as otherwise required to get into colleges and universities, which will then result in lowered expectations of college graduates and decreased credibility of college diplomas.

首先，當台灣的生育率持續下滑，且沒有好轉的跡象時，將會造成日後學生數的短缺，這將嚴重威脅到剩餘的大學，因為大家都知道，大學的營運就如同企業一樣，都需要資金及相當的資源以求生存，而即將出現的學生數量短缺也代表了學費、資金的短缺，最終將迫使許多大學別無選擇而倒閉，另外，過多的高等教育學府將使入學變得過於簡易，反而使社會對於畢業大學生的期望降低，也將對於大學文憑的可信度產生質疑。

As ubiquitous as colleges and universities are today, government should be thinking about how to effectively phase out redundant institutions. Now these institutions are like a drop in the ocean, as too many of them are offered yet not enough demand in return.

如同今日隨處可見的大學設立，政府應思考該如何有效地安排過多的大學退場，因目前大學車載斗量，實在是供過於求。

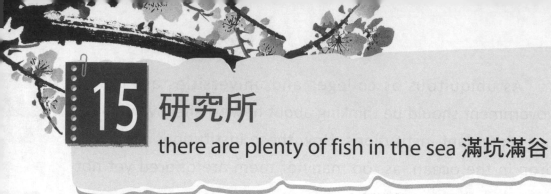

15 研究所
there are plenty of fish in the sea 滿坑滿谷

成語閱讀故事

　　成語「滿坑滿谷」與「車載斗量」的意思相近，皆可用來形容某件事的數量極多，其出處來自《莊子‧天運》：「在谷滿倉，在坑滿坑。」，本是指莊子所倡導的「道」的實施，及其運行是無所不在的，後演變、引申為用來形容數量極多、多到坑與谷都將溢滿出來；在英文中，可用「there are plenty of fish in the sea」這句話來形容某個事物的數量龐大，經常用於鼓勵、安慰別人的談話中，指出某個事物因無所不在，不用因為失去一次機會而感到氣餒，因其「滿坑滿谷」，還有許多其它的機會可以把握。

In Taiwan, there are a plethora of graduate schools at college graduates' finger tips as Taiwan places much emphasis on a person's educational experience.

This has driven many college graduates to enter one of the many graduate schools right after graduation. This in turn generates many more graduate schools for this demand.

However, there have been quite a few heated arguments among critics as to this social phenomenon, debating whether it is truly beneficial for the society to churn out so many graduates with a master's degree?

Please show your stance on this and explain.

寫作技巧解析

　　題目説道，台灣屬於亞洲社會，因此重視一個人的學歷及文憑，也因此有許多大學畢業的學生選擇繼續進入研究所研讀、攻取碩士學位，而也因為有此需求，研究所的設立也越來越普遍，最後詢問考生是否贊同大學畢業生一窩蜂地進入研究所就讀的社會現象；以下範文採反對立場，並用「there are plenty of fish in the sea」來形容研究所的普遍，並説明可在進入職場工作、較瞭解自身興趣後，再決定是否要讀研究所也不遲。

應試撇步

　　「研究所」的英文可用「graduate school」或是「postgraduate school」兩種説法，而在第二段中，使用了「well-versed」這個形容詞來説明研究生較專攻於學術方面，而對於現實生活中知識的運用，並不如台灣社會所預想地「熟稔」，而最後結尾時，重申大學畢業生應謹慎「評估 weigh」所有的「優缺點 pros and cons」，再「謹慎小心地進行 proceed with caution」，以免浪費時間。

 作文範例

In Taiwan, college graduates are highly encouraged to try out for graduate schools. The society in general views those who have completed a master's degree in a favorable light. However, I do not support the mentality of placing postgraduate education in such a high regard as Taiwan's society does.

在台灣，大學畢業生常被鼓勵繼續求學、攻讀研究所，整體社會觀點認為有研究所學位是一件好的事情，然而，我並不贊同如台灣社會如此地重視、看好取得碩士學位的心態。

First, it is important to understand that the purpose of postgraduate education is supposed to be about academic exploration. However, many Taiwanese view someone's completion of a postgraduate degree synonymous with someone being workplace ready. It is especially ironic as many business entities in Taiwan only give out interview opportunities to candidates with master's degrees. It is ironic because those who spend much time completing a master's degree are mostly academically trained rather than well-versed in the real-world operations of whichever specialization they are exploring. As a matter of fact, years of academic studies towards garnering a master's degree may not truly benefit individuals in the long run, unless their career aspiration is to

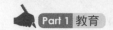

become an established scholar in their chosen fields of study. Secondly, the increase in the supply of graduate schools to meet the corresponding demand will make the process of finishing graduate programs less special, and soon graduating from a postgraduate school will just be a formality since everyone else is doing the same without great difficulty. Lastly, college graduates are often unsure as to what their real interests are, and graduates should test the waters in the real world and get back to school for postgraduate studies when they have a better gauge on their interests.

　　首先，我們必須了解碩士教育的重點在於學術的探討，然而，許多台灣人將碩士學位的取得與職場工作的表現視為同一件事，而當台灣的許多企業在徵才時只考慮有碩士學位的求職者時，令人感到格外地諷刺，因為這些取得碩士學位的學生們，花了許多時間在學術的訓練上，但對於他們學位專科在現實生活中的運用，並沒有相對應的熟稔度，若不是要成為學者，或純粹地想要更深入探討某一學科領域，攻讀碩士學位或許並不如台灣社會所想的，並不是對於將知識應用於現實生活中般有幫助的；第二，為了應付攻讀研究所的需求，研究所的廣泛增設，將使攻讀研究所這件事平凡化，而最終也將使攻讀研究所流於形式，只因為大家都在讀。最後，因為許多大學畢業生還無法知道自己的興趣為何，所以大學畢業生應當在現實世界中多加嘗試，在更瞭解自己的性向、興趣之後，再回去攻讀也不遲。

Based on the above arguments, I oppose the idea of going into postgraduate studies immediately after college. As there are plenty of fish in the sea, people should carefully weigh the pros and cons of having a master's degree, and proceed with caution so that no time is unnecessarily wasted.

　　根據以上的論述，我反對大學畢業後直接進入研究所攻取學位，也因為有著滿坑滿谷的研究所，人們應當審慎思考攻讀碩士學位的優缺點，才不會浪費不必要的時間。

16 出國留學
quality over quantity 兵在精，不在多

成語閱讀故事

　　成語「兵在精，不在多」，其字面上的意思是在形容，若要贏得一場戰爭，士兵的整體素質比數量還要來的重要，並不是數量多就好，士兵的整體質量要優質才行，才會更有打勝仗的機率，而這個道理，也可延伸運用至生活、社會中的各個層面，說明很多時候，品質的確是比數量還要重要的道理；在英文中，時常聽到「quality over quantity」這句話，其所說的正是「兵在精，不在多」的道理，簡單來說，也就是品質大於數量的意思。

寫作題目

In the Taiwanese society, graduating from prestigious schools is one of the many sought-after pursuits that parents encourage students to strive for.

This is even more so if the diploma is earned from an overseas institution since the society generally holds the idea that people who graduate from an overseas institution, no matter which school they go to, are stronger job candidates in terms of their language abilities, expansive thinking in a global context and so on.

However, many argue that this is not true most of the time. What people learn at an educational institution is a far cry from what is realistically practiced in the real business world. What is your take on this? Please explain.

寫作技巧解析

　　題目提到，台灣社會的觀念，認為從名校畢業的學生，尤其是帶有國外留學的光環的學生，整體來說在找工作或是職涯的發展上，將更具競爭力，因為社會認為這些學生擁有語言的優勢、國際觀等等，然而，現今社會中也出現反對的意見，認為此說法不盡正確；以下範文採取支持反對的立場，認為學歷的多寡並不是最重要的，反而是在學校所學得的技能，比是否擁有碩博士的學位來得重要多了，因為「兵在精，不在多 quality over quantity」。

應試撇步

　　範文提到，台灣社會中許多民眾有「錯誤的認知 misconception」，認為國外「高等教育 higher education」的文憑「等同於 equate to」較好的職涯發展以及高薪待遇，然而事實上並非如此，而當社會太過於「高估 overestimate」這些文憑所帶來的利益時，畢業生面對畢業後的「全新局面 a whole new ball game」才「清醒、認清事實 in for a rude awakening」時，這對於社會的發展是沒有助益的，也因此，社會中個人所受教育的多寡，的確不比其在學校所受教育的品質，及其教育所提供他面對社會、職場上的適應能力還要來得重要。

 作文範例　🔘 MP3 016

　　In the Taiwanese society, many people have the misconception of what a higher education degree earned overseas can equip the graduate with. Many believe that graduating from a prestigious school in a foreign country automatically equates to a better job prospect and higher salary pay. Nevertheless, this is not true in reality. Many graduates with degrees of higher education are in for a rude awakening as they enter the job market fresh off school. One reason behind such a shock felt by fresh new graduates is the fact that there is a fine distinction between scholarly studies and real-world ways of doing business. Therefore, I am in agreement with not holding the amount of people's education history in too high of regard, but rather on how much they are able to demonstrate their practical skills for the business.

　　在台灣的社會中，許多人認為國外的高教育文憑，能夠對其畢業生帶來許多的助益，儘管這種認知並不是這麼地正確，但的確還是有許多人相信，若能夠從國外的名校畢業，將能夠自然而然地找到好的工作及高薪待遇，然而，這些期待與事實並不相符，許多具有高等教育文憑的畢業生，在剛畢業找工作時，才認清社會職場現實面，而背後的原因之一在於學校所教導、探討的學術面，與現實社會中的商業環境有所差別，因此，我同意不要將一個人的學歷多寡看得太重，反而，應當著重在一個人能夠如何地展現自己的實務能力。

As with many things in life, quality over quantity is the way to go. However, as the society has been for years blindly overestimating the benefits that come with higher education, people are easily given the wrong impression of how educations play such an integral role in determining how well of they are going to be when entering the job market. They, especially youngsters, are not aware of how it is a whole new ball game when they are starting a career. Oftentimes, you need to work yourself up the corporate ladder on the merits of practical experience, rather than one's education background.

正如生活中的許多事物，兵在精，不在多，然而，當社會多年來盲目地高估高等教育對學生所帶來的益處時，人們容易有個錯誤的觀念，認為教育在學生日後的職涯發展、成功上，扮演了不可或缺的角色，但許多年輕人並未及早發覺職場與學校的教育是很不同的，因為很多時候，攀爬企業階級所需要的是實務經驗，而不是靠一個人的學歷背景。

In short, with the above said, I feel the amount of education is not as important as its quality, in terms of how well people are properly trained and prepared for the real world. Thus, I oppose the overstated hype placed on the amount of education by the Taiwanese society.

根據以上論述,簡單來說,一個人的學歷多寡,還不如其所受的教育品質,也就是他們對於進入社會、職場的準備程度還來得重要,因此,我反對台灣社會對於教育多寡過度著重的現象。

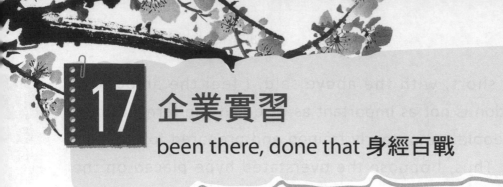

17 企業實習
been there, done that 身經百戰

成語閱讀故事

　　成語「身經百戰」字面上的意思是指某人歷經過許多的戰役，引申用來形容某人因歷經過許多大大小小的事情，所以在遇到困難或挑戰時能夠臨危不亂，不容易被驚動；在英文中，可用「been there, done that」來形容某人對於某事很有經驗，也正因為有過親身的體驗，對於同樣的事物更能夠以平常心來看待，所以此諺語在用法及意思上來說，與中文成語「身經百戰」類似，皆是用來形容對於某事物很有經驗、體悟的人。

寫作題目

Around the world, it is quite prevalent for students to get internship at companies of various sizes, just to acquire some hands-on experiences.

A lot of the times, students are offered very little salaries, sometimes even none. Still, many would be eager to jump at those internship opportunities, yearning to gain more real life experiences in the business world.

Some may argue that such a phenomenon is an exploit on the innocent and naïve, while others may argue that the experiences that these interns are having are simply invaluable.

What is your take on this? Please elaborate on your stance.

1 教育

2 社會法律議題

3 民生生活

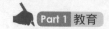

⊕ 寫作技巧解析

　　以下範文將以正面、支持的立場，來闡述為何學生應當把握在企業實習的機會；首先，會提及到在學校就讀的學子們，因為環境的關係，對於整個社會及企業的運作，或者是基本的人際關係，是還比較生澀的，而這些技巧及道理是需要親身經歷、體驗，才能夠真正有所領悟的，並在最後說道，有這些企業實習經驗的年輕人，在日後的職涯、人生發展上，由於歷經過的事物較豐富，皆已「身經百戰 been there, done that」了。

⑥ 應試撇步

　　第一段中提到企業實習生通常是給付「最低工資 minimum wage」，甚至有些還「不給薪」，用「nonpayment」這個名詞來敘說；而在第二段，一開始用「internalize」這個動詞，來說人「內化」身邊的經驗、所學等等這個動作，並用「extract」來描述學生自己來「擷取」出對於自己日後正式出社會後有益的心得、感想等，最後也用另一句諺語「make lemonade out of lemons」來說明就算企業實習的經驗不美好，個人還是能夠思考、擷取出值得帶走的經驗、課題。

 作文範例 　　　　　　　　　　　　MP3 017

　　Around the globe, it has been quite popular for students to try out internship opportunities. Despite the fact that they are often just being offered a minimum wage, and sometimes even face nonpayment, many of them are still more than happy to spend time devoting energy and expertise to companies who are willing to give them a chance. Some may argue that students tend to be exploited by enterprises that they end up not only getting paid miserably but also learning minimal things. I personally take the opposite stance against such claims, and support youngsters to seek internship opportunities wherever possible.

　　在這世界上，學生們流行去申請企業實習的機會，儘管企業實習的薪水通常是基本薪資，甚至有時是不給薪的，很多學生還是樂意花時間效勞於願意給他們實習機會的企業，而有些人會認為這些學生極有可能淪為被企業利用的勞工，最終不僅薪資給配少，又學習有限，而我個人並不認同此種論點，並支持年輕人盡量追求企業實習的機會。

To begin with, any experience is good experience. It is up to individuals to internalize whatever situations they find themselves in, and extract something useful from them to go with so that they are better prepared when later on inevitably facing challenges in life. As the school environment is vastly different from the cutthroat business world, they should really get themselves exposed, and gain first-hand insights into how businesses operate, how people interact with each other in a professional setting, and so on. Granted, not all experiences would be pleasant, especially when monetary rewards for these internship positions are typically minimal. Still, those who make lemonade out of lemons can still bring invaluable lessons from which they are in touch with during their internship programs.

首先，任何的經驗皆是好的經驗，端看個人如何內化自身的經驗，並擷取出對於日後人生中無可避免的挑戰，些許有用的心得及感想。而也因為學校的環境與社會險惡的環境差距甚遠，他們更應該盡量接觸、探索瞭解企業的運作方式，以及商務人士於專業情境中應如何互動等等。當然，不可能所有的實習經驗都是正面、美好的，尤其當實習生的給配是如此微薄時，但是，能夠在負面經驗中擷取正面學習經驗的學生，仍是能在最後帶走寶貴的經驗。

In summary, those who take the time to equip themselves with hands-on experiences through internship can learn a great deal, and thus be ahead of the game when compared to their peers. In other word, those who have been there and done that, would have a head start on the lessons learned through internship.

大致來說，願意花時間體驗、親身學習的學生能夠學習到許多東西，也因此能夠在起跑線領先同儕；換句話說，那些身經百戰的學生，能夠藉由企業實習贏在起跑點。

18 打工度假

He that travels far knows much 讀萬卷書，行萬里路

成語閱讀故事

　　成語「讀萬卷書，行萬里路」原是用來形容人追求知識的最高境界，不僅在學術方面，能夠廣泛地涉及、閱讀各家書冊，而在生活方面，也能夠到處遊覽、開拓自身的眼界，而隨著時代的演進，此成語也間接發展出另一番意涵，開始有了「讀萬卷書不如行萬里路」的用法，所指的是在外頭開拓自身的視野、人生經歷，比關在象牙塔裡猛讀上萬書冊，還要能夠拓展一個人的思維；在英文中，可用諺語「He that travels far knows much.」來形容相同的意涵，鼓勵人們多出去闖，吸取、見識生活中的不同層面及智慧。

寫作題目

In many parts of the world, youngsters may value and opt for working holiday opportunities offered by other countries.

By definition, working holiday visas allow people to work overseas, mostly at jobs that are more labor-intensive.

On the other hand, they are also given a chance to see more of the world with this visa. As this phenomenon is gaining the momentum within younger generations, some take the opposing stance and argue that it is not only demeaning, but a waste of time for youngsters to spend time working at labor-intensive jobs in foreign countries.

What is your stance on this? Please explain.

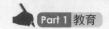

寫作技巧解析

　　題目說道「打工度假」在全球蔚為流行，許多年輕人想藉由此工作賺錢的機會，順道在世界不同的角落旅遊、觀光，然而有些人對此卻抱持著反對的意見，認為「打工度假」的背後，其實是讓年輕人到別的國家從事較勞力密集的產業、工作，並不是一件有意義的事；以下範文採正面支持立場，並以「He that travels far knows much.」這句諺語，來鼓勵年輕人多出去走走、闖蕩，因為「讀萬卷書，行萬里路」，多接觸世界上不同的角落、事物，是能夠拓展視野的。

應試撇步

　　範文在一段中有提到，會去打工度假的人，經常「是為了 for the purpose of」金錢的誘惑，而除了金錢的誘惑，還有能夠「充實人生 life-enriching」的體驗，因為在異地打工度假，無可避免地將會迫使人「跳脫舒適圈 step out of the comfort zone」，而也正因為脫離舒適、習以為常的環境，才能夠成長，而在最後一段總結時，使用本單元的諺語來一語概括本文的論述。

 作文範例　　MP3 018

In today's world, it is quite common for youngsters to apply for a working holiday visa and to land in a foreign country with the sole purpose of two things: money and travel. Although those aspiring travelers tend to find themselves in the employment of industries that are typically labeled labor-intensive, they would still gladly take the deal as these jobs can sometimes yield a considerably larger amount of money than they could possibly get from working in their own countries. Therefore, I do not agree with statements that hold an opposing view on today's prevalent working holiday applications that are filed by our younger generation.

　　今日有許多的年輕人選擇申請打工度假簽證，而他們到別的國家打工的目的有兩個：金錢和旅遊，而儘管他們在別的國家經常是在勞動力較密集的產業打工，他們仍然很樂意在這些工作上打拼，因為這些工作所給予的薪資，是比他們在自己國家所能賺取的還要多的，因此，那些對於今日年輕世代踴躍申請打工度假簽證的現象，持否定觀點的人的意見，我並不贊同。

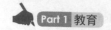

There are two aspects to this situation: one is monetary and the other would be life-enriching experiences. As mentioned in the last paragraph, the monetary rewards of working holiday opportunities are usually tremendous, although it goes without saying that these rewards are earned through hard work as well. Also, people can broaden their horizons when working in foreign, unfamiliar countries. When abroad, they are exposed to many things that are unfamiliar, unheard of, or not even thought of. What's more, they need to depend on themselves when facing unexpected challenges in a foreign country. All these, without a doubt, will ultimately contribute to growth that is derived from these life-enriching experiences.

目前的情況有兩個方面值得討論：金錢及充實人生經歷的體驗，如在上段所提及的，打工度假機會所提供的金錢酬勞是很龐大的，當然於工作上所付出的精力也是相對辛苦的，然而，除了金錢，那些嘗試打工度假的人常發現他們的視野開闊了，因為打工度假讓他們必須跳脫舒適圈，且當在國外時，他們會經歷許多不熟悉、沒聽過，甚至是從沒想過會發生的事情，而當在國外面對無預期的挑戰時，他們必須依靠自己。這些，無庸置疑地，將使他們從這些充實人生經歷的體驗中成長。

With Above-mentioned arguments combined, it seems that the saying "he that travels far knows much" is true. Those who have chosen working holiday opportunities as part of their life course are the true testament to this saying, and that is why I support people taking actions on this.

綜合上述，諺語説的「讀萬卷書，行萬里路」似乎是真的。那些選擇讓打工度假成為他們人生旅途中之一的景點的人，正是此諺語的最佳驗證，因此我支持、鼓勵人們嘗試打工度假。

1

教育

2

社會法律議題

3

民生生活

part**2**

社會
法律
議題

1 廢除死刑

There are two sides to every question 公說公有理，婆說婆有理

成語閱讀故事

　　成語「公說公有理，婆說婆有理」的意思是指對於同一件事情，雙方僵持不下，堅持認為自己的看法及理論是對的，而在英文中，有句諺語叫作「There are two sides to every question」，其字面上的意思是指一個錢幣有兩面，引申的意思即為同樣一件事情，無可避免地必定有兩個不同的觀點、正反面向，意思與成語「公說公有理，婆說婆有理」相近，而在本單元中，可用來形容台灣在死刑存廢這個議題上，不同團體以不同的觀點來看待其存廢的現象。

寫作題目

In Taiwan, there have been multiple heated discussions on whether death penalty should be abolished or not.

There are social groups urging for the abolition of death penalty, while on the other hand there are those who strongly oppose the idea of abolishing this penalty.

For the social groups, they urge the abolition from more of a humanitarian standpoint. On the contrary, the opposing side fears the abolition would somehow become some sort of encouragement for committing serious crimes without corresponding consequences holding those offenders accountable.

Which side do you agree with on the abolition of death penalty in Taiwan? Please explain.

寫作技巧解析

　　題目說道，台灣社會目前對於廢除死刑這個議題，有著不同的想法，有些社運團體抱持著支持廢除死刑的觀點，但也有許多人反對廢除死刑，認為死刑若廢除的話，將會無形中鼓舞社會中犯罪情事的增長，因為司法將失去有效仲裁的方式；以下範文在第一段中先提到「公說公有理，婆說婆有理 There are two side to every question」，來概述台灣社會目前對於廢除死刑這個議題上所持有的不同看法。

應試撇步

　　本範文一開頭便先點出台灣社會目前對於廢除死刑，存在著正反兩面的看法，並在第二段提到這幾年接二連三發生的「隨機殺人事件 random killing」，而司法無法在第一個重大隨機殺人案發生後的第一時間執行有效制裁，引發了「摸仿效應 the Imitation Effect」，而從某個角度來看，之後所發生的案件，可說是第一起案件的「副產物 byproduct」。

 作文範例　　　　　　　　　　🔊 MP3 019

　　In Taiwan, there have been contentious debates on whether the death penalty should be abolished or not. As with anything, there are always two sides to every question. Both the supporting side and the opposing side on the continued existence of the death penalty will make strong arguments to defend their stance. From my personal point of view, I concur with the reasoning of the opposing side as I find their arguments more compelling and logical, and will explain further in the next paragraph.

　　台灣最近有許多激烈的辯論，討論死刑是否應該廢除，而正如許多事情一樣，總是公說公有理，婆說婆有理，而正反兩方對於死刑的存廢都有各自的論點，至於我個人的觀點來看，我較同意反方所持的論點，因為我認為反方的論點較強烈、符合邏輯，而在下一段會更加詳細說明。

To begin with, there have been a couple of incidents where manslaughter is carried out in the broad daylight in Taiwan. The fact that the criminals responsible are not executed immediately after arrest is not only adding insult to injury, but also creating the Imitation Effect. Since the first incident of random killing took place, the following episodes of similar offences are considered a byproduct of the first incidence. In fact, many people actually blame the Imitation Effect a result of the legal system's lack of warranted punishment on the first offender in a timely manner. Therefore, it is important to point out that since the pure delay of proper execution on offenders could have ramifications on the whole society, the abolition of the death penalty is for sure to have a bigger impact.

首先，台灣最近有一連串於公開場合殺人的事件，而當這些罪犯並沒有於逮捕後的第一時間處以相關責任刑罰時，不只使事情雪上加霜，也產生了模仿效應，自從第一起隨機殺人事件發生後，隨後發生的類似案件可被視為第一起案件的副產物，而事實上，許多人譴責司法系統所缺乏的即時處罰、判決機制，造就了這波模仿效應，因此，我們必須瞭解到，若單純司法處罰、判決的延遲，就能夠對於整個社會產生許多影響，那死刑的廢除更是不用說了。

In summary, the abolition of the death penalty, though might be viewed humanitarian in the eye of some social groups, would ultimately alter the dynamics of social justice system. To avoid that, I oppose to abolish such punishment for major crime offences.

總結來說，儘管有些社運團體認為廢除死刑是人道的，但終將會對社會正義系統造成影響，而若要避免此影響，我反對廢除死刑。

1 教育

2 社會法律議題

3 民生生活

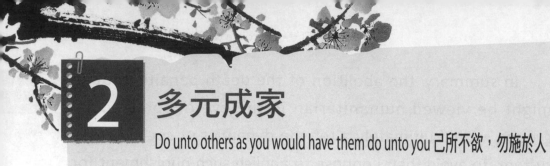

2 多元成家

Do unto others as you would have them do unto you 己所不欲，勿施於人

成語閱讀故事

　　成語「己所不欲，勿施於人」其出處來自於論語，當孔子的學徒子貢詢問孔子：「有哪一句話，可以作為終身奉行的圭臬呢？」，孔子以「恕」這個字為核心價值，以「己所不欲，勿施於人」這句話來闡述其背後倡行的精神，對子貢說明對於自己個人所不欣賞、不喜好的行為，應當避免施加於他人，這就是人生活上應當奉行的圭臬、準則；在英文中，也有類似相對應的智慧箴言，是出自聖經的「Do unto others as you would have them do unto you」，簡單來說，也就是以同理心待人，以你期望被對待的方式來待人。

寫作題目

In many parts of the world, the LGBT community is advocating for their rights pertaining to legal marriage, desiring what is essentially argued as the basic human right.

In fact, they are asking for the legality of marriage, which has been granted to couples of man and woman for centuries. However, there are many pushbacks from a variety of sources, mainly the religious groups, stating that same-sex marriages are a blunt violation to their observed religious doctrines. Also, there're other factors at play, such as some traditional values that are deep-rooted in certain societies than others.

What is your stance on the legality of same-sex issues? Do you think marriages outside the conventional form of one male and one female should be legalized? Please explain.

寫作技巧解析

題目說道，LGBT(Lesbian, Gay, Bi-sexual, Transgender)社群團體在世界各地爭取其婚姻合法化，儘管有些人認為合法結婚的權利，應屬基本人權，但也有許多反對的聲浪，諸如宗教、社會傳統觀點等因素，使得多元成家的議題如此具有爭議；以下範文採取支持多元成家的正面立場，並於第二段帶出本單元成語「Do unto others as you would have them do unto you」支撐其論點。

應試撇步

本文一開始用片語「*tie the knot*」來討論多元「成家」的合法性，而一般的多元成家，廣泛來說涵蓋了整個 LGBT 社群，而其中比較常見的形式為「同性婚姻 same-sex marriage」；第二段文章主體解釋，聖經中提道「Do unto others as you would have them do unto you 己所不欲，勿施於人」，若異性戀「被剝奪 stripped of」婚姻的合法性，必然也是會感到不悅，且性傾向的成因也還無法確認，有人宣稱是「由基因來判定 genetically determined」，若是這樣而因為天生的原因無法結婚，是不公平的。

 作文範例

MP3 020

In recent years, the right to legally tie the knot for the LGBT community has starting to gain a stronger footing in certain parts of the world. However, there's still much room for improvement when it comes to the right being universal around the world. There are some constraints for such a right to be universally legalized by the community. These constraints are mainly backed by the religious doctrines and traditional values that depict same-sex marriages as unsanctified. I personally hold the view of legalizing same-sex marriages and the sort as something that should be passed and granted to the community, and will explain why in the following paragraph.

在最近幾年內，LGBT 社群結婚的法定權益已在世界的某些地方漸漸地獲得重視，但是各地方在追求婚姻一視同仁的進展上，仍有許多進步的空間，而其阻礙的來源，主要來自宗教教條及傳統社會價值，因其將同性婚姻描繪為褻瀆神聖的；而我個人的觀感認為，同性婚姻等非傳統的結合應當受到法律保護，而原因會於下一段詳述。

First of all, despite the fact that much of the opposition is fueled by religious beliefs, it is ironic that the quote "Do unto others as you would have them do unto you" comes straight from the bible. This quote essentially explains why I stand in favor of the legalization of same-sex marriages, as heterosexual individuals much enjoy their given right to legally marry their significant others and would be much upset if stripped of that given privilege. In that thread of thought, individuals from the LGBT community should enjoy the same. Secondly, it is not scientifically conclusive as to why individuals are attracted to the same sex. Some posit that sexual orientations are genetically determined, and it is unfair to be stripped of their legal right based on the way they are born and brought to the world.

首先，儘管許多反對的聲浪來自宗教的信仰，諷刺的是聖經中卻倡導著「己所不欲，勿施於人」的觀念，而這個觀念也正是我支持同性婚姻合法化的原因，正如異性戀個體正當享受與另一半合法結婚的權益，若被剝奪此權益將會感到極度沮喪，因此，LGBT 社群個體也應當享有相同的權益；第二點，科學家還無法確切地瞭解性傾向的影響因素，有些推測性傾向是由基因所決定的，而因為天生的性傾向而遭剝奪相關的權益是不公平的。

In summary, I strongly hold the view of supporting the legality of the same-sex marriages. As stated above, it is unfair to take away people's right to marry their beloved ones, irrespective of which sex they are romantically attracted to.

總結來說，我全面支持同性婚姻的合法性，正如以上所述，不論性取向，將任何人與其所愛的人合法結婚的權益剝奪，都是件不公平的情事。

1 教育

2 社會法律議題

3 民生生活

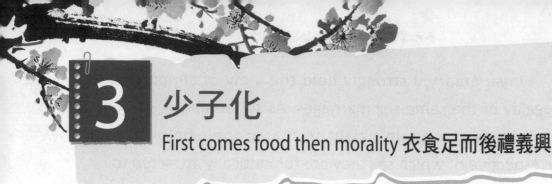

3 少子化

First comes food then morality 衣食足而後禮義興

成語閱讀故事

　　諺語「衣食足而後禮義興」，原本是指一個國家須先將人民的基本生活起居照顧好，至少能讓人民不餓肚子、不憂愁穿著等基本的民生用品，才能進展到下一個境界，也就是才能開始談論如何提升人民基本的道德水準等精神層面的指標，簡單來說就是形容一個人須要先解決基本的生活需求，才能談論精神、道德層面的提升；在英文中，有句知名的話語「First comes food then morality」，形容的即是這個要點，需要先有足夠的食物滿足基本生理需求，才能開始討論道德的建構。

Not only in Taiwan, but around the developed countries of the world, the trend towards people having fewer children is growing and becoming ever more prominent.

In Taiwan, the government is showing concerns and comes up with a variety of incentive programs aimed at birth-rate boosting. In the media, economists constantly issue warnings against the declining birth rate as a major cause for potential economic collapse.

On the flipside, people are choosing to have fewer children with an assortment of rationales behind the choice.

What is your take on such a social phenomenon? Please state and explain your opinions on this.

寫作技巧解析

　　題目說道，不只在台灣，其實在全世界眾多已開發國家中，少子化的趨勢已越來越明顯、主流化，而台灣政府已開始祭出眾多激勵生育的各式方案，以求能夠提升生育率，然而民眾對於生育孩子的想法也已隨著時代改變；以下範文採取支持少子化的立場，並以諺語「衣食足而後禮義興 First comes food then morality」支撐立場，說明在現代注重生活品質的年代，質大於量，將一個家裡的資源集中在少數孩子的教育上，對於整個國家的提升是有幫助的。

應試撇步

　　範文提到，有關全球少子化的現象，各地國家、社會如何因應、應對，是「極度、非常重要的 of paramount importance」，而隨著經濟發展，少子化現象也帶來了人類對於生活品質要求的提升，不像古時候，或較早年代時的人們，習慣過著「節儉的 frugal」的生活，其主要是因為少子化的現象減少了許多家庭的負擔，讓現代的孩子們能夠充分地享有足夠的資源，不需與「手足、兄弟姊妹 siblings」分享家中的資源，也因此間接提高了現代人對於生活水準標準的提升。

 作文範例   MP3 021

　　When it comes to discussions pertaining to the developing trend in declining birth rates around the world, I do not hold a negative view on such an issue. Rather, I think it is how the society, as a whole, deals with such an issue that should be taken into serious considerations. After all, as the world is collectively getting more developed and civilized over the passage of time, the trend in declining birth rates shall turn out to be irreversible. As a result, how societies respond to fewer children being born to the world is of paramount importance. What's more, I think there are quite a few timely opportunities that can be taken advantage of during this period for the progression of society as a whole.

　　有關世界各地少子化的現象，我並不秉持負面的觀點，反而，我認為整體社會應當好好考量當面對此議題時，該如何面對？畢竟，當整體來說，世界越加走向已開發、文明的發展時，少子化的趨勢是很難逆轉的。因此，社會應對少子化的方式是極度重要的，而我也認為，若能夠於此時把握因少子化趨勢而衍生出來的機會，整體社會福祉將能夠改善、提升。

As the saying goes, "First comes food then morality." As the level of living standards are lifted with the development of countries and societies, a certain kind of life style has come into place that would not be easily replaced by the older ways of living; that is, a more frugal way. Fewer children being born can lessen economic burdens on families. In turn, they can then have more access to available resources in the family, with no need to share or divide those resources with siblings.

正如諺語「衣食足而後禮義興」所說的,當生活水準與社會、國家的發展一同提升時,生活水平將發展至一定的境界,而過往、古早時代較為節省的生活方式將難以被新世代接受,而少子化的現象也將減少各個家庭的負擔,因為孩子們不必再跟兄弟姊妹爭取家庭裡有限的資源。

In a nutshell, despite cautions and warnings by scholars regarding the declining birth rates, I do think when dealt right, people are going to enjoy a higher quality of life due to individuals' increased access to limited resources on offer. Therefore, I am not against the declining rate.

概括來説，儘管許多學者警告少子化趨勢可能帶來的衝擊，我認為只要正確應對，人們將可享有更高水平的生活水準，因為每個人將可於有限的資源內享有更多，所以我並不排斥少子化的趨勢。

1 教育

2 社會法律議題

3 民生生活

4 高齡化
go begging 乏人問津

📖 成語閱讀故事

　　成語「乏人問津」所形容的是極少人對於某件事感到有興趣，而因為沒有興趣，所以詢問相關事物的人是非常少、幾近零的；英文有句常用的片語「**go begging**」，雖然其主流用法是用來稱讚某人能言善道、業務能力極佳，能夠賣冰塊給愛斯基摩人，但在本單元範文裡，將會以「**go begging**」來延伸、帶出「乏人問津」的意涵，形容在高齡化的社會中，某些企業若不採取相對應措施，以高齡族群為目標客群，會產生社會對於其產品「乏人問津」的現象。

寫作題目

In today's world, societies appear to be aging in terms of demographics. This is especially true in developed countries where birth rates have been on the trend of declining.

The declining birth rates would have serious ramifications on the development of societies. For instance, the declining birth rates would have a serious impact on businesses that have not entered the so-called senior market.

What are your thoughts on the phenomenon pertaining to businesses that have not entered the market for older demographics?

Do you agree with businesses stay clear of the market or do you think they should expand into the market? Please explain your thoughts.

 寫作技巧解析

　　題目提到，在現今的世界中，社會高齡化的現象日趨明顯，尤其是在已開發、生育率較低的國家，而這個現象對社會帶來了許多的影響，其中商業正是受影響的很大一部分，尤其是對於原本並無打算進軍高齡市場的企業，其影響更是不言可喻；以下範文採支持企業積極應變、進軍高齡市場的立場，以免錯過時機，當市場上對其產品「乏人問津 go begging」，才後悔莫及。

⑥ 應試撇步

　　範文提到，在整體「老化的 aging」社會中，「敏銳的 acute」企業家皆開始考量老化市場的需求，深怕若沒有求新求變，最終將失去企業的競爭力；範文並以一個「假設的 hypothetical」企業為例，說明若其主要的販賣商品只包括嬰兒用品的話，其「前景 prospect」將不被看好，因此求新求變的心態對於企業來說是很重樣的。

作文範例

As societies are aging with their demographics, acute business owners and management team should be thinking about how to best adapt to the aging environment to avoid being eliminated out of business due to a lack of customers. This is even more urgent for businesses that have not even planned any sort of entry into the market for elders. In my opinion, it is simply imperative for businesses to always be in the mindset of evolving and adapting to market changes. Shortly speaking, in today's business climate, enterprises ought to constantly reinvent themselves, and one way to do so is to consider the needs of the senior market in their strategy sessions.

當社會人口老化時，機警的公司所有人及管理團隊應當思考該如何應變，才不至於因為沒有足夠業績而被淘汰，而對於還沒計畫搶攻高齡市場的企業來說，這更應當成為該企業的當務之急，就我來看，任何企業原本就應該隨時保持在更新、改變的狀態，而處在高齡化社會的企業，若尚未計畫進軍高齡市場，更應當盡快思考如何創新求變、搶攻此市場。

For example, if a business is now mainly in baby amenities business, what the prospects are going to look like after a few years passing? As the birth rates are just ever going to be on a downward slope, whereas the age average for society demographics is on an upward slope, the hypothetical business would most likely to go under if it does not react quickly enough to the aging component of the business environment. In other words, this business would go begging as elders would find no use for baby amenities. Therefore, adaptation and changing tactics for businesses are the strongly recommended.

舉例來說，若一個企業的主要業務為銷售嬰兒用品，這個企業幾年後未來的前景將如何呢？當社會中的出生率下降、社會平均年齡上升，這個假設的企業很有可能會被淘汰，倘若其不做出即時、適當的改變的話；換句話說，這個企業最後於市場上將會乏人問津，因為老化的人口多半會對於嬰兒用品毫無興趣，因此，企業改變及調整策略將是生存之道。

In conclusion, running a business is tough, and the market place is always fickle and fierce for the game of the survival of the fittest. The best tactic for businesses may be to start incorporating senior customers into considerations when devising annual market strategies.

總結來說，企業營運是艱難的，而營運市場總是變化萬千、競爭激烈，上演著適者生存的遊戲，而最好的應變方式，或許就是於編制年度計畫時，開始將高齡市場納入考量範圍內。

1 教育

2 社會法律議題

3 民生生活

5 安樂死
Circle of Life 有生必有死

 成語閱讀故事

　　諺語「有生必有死」所形容的即是人生中個體必經的過程，有新生命的誕生，也必然就有生命的逝去，這是百年不變的道理，也形成、架構出宇宙生生不息的結構，被生命的週期所串聯起來；在英文中，迪士尼經典卡通「獅子王」裡有個著名的歌曲「Circle of Life」，其簡單一句話，即描繪了宇宙中的平衡法則，這也就是亙古至今永恆不變的循環週期，而這也是具有正面能量的一句話，可用於新生兒到臨喜悅的祝福，而有時也用來正面看待去世、辭世這件事情。

寫作題目

Globally, the ethical issue of euthanasia is controversial and is surrounded by heated conversations involving interested parties.

Among the opposition forces, religious groups feel strongly against the practice of euthanasia. They fight against the given choice and power to individuals in ending life on their own term. These groups piously adhere to the doctrines of their religious beliefs, and argue that only God can decide when to end one's own life.

However, how about people who are chronically ill with no potential recovery in sight?

Should they be given the choice and power in deciding if they should end their own lives? Please share your stance on euthanasia and explain.

寫作技巧解析

　　題目提到，安樂死的道德議題在全球極具爭議性，而其中主要的反對者為宗教團體，因為他們認為只有上帝才有權決定一個人該何時離開這個世上，但題目也提到，若有些人不幸患上難以復原的絕症，是否應當有權決定自身的生死？以下範文採取支持安樂死的立場，並以「有生必有死 circle of life」的觀點，理性來淡看生死議題。

應試撇步

　　本範文表示支持「安樂死 euthanasia」的施行，但是應在病患實際處於健康「無法復原 irrecoverable」的狀態下，因為若只是靠醫療器材來「支撐 sustain」病患的「基本生理功能 basic bodily function」的話，其實是沒有意義的，不僅病患本身不願意，也會造成其家屬過多的負擔，包含了「累積的經濟負擔 accumulated economic expenses」以及「體力及精力 physical and mental energy」；最後總結時，點出生與死只是自然的一部分，應當理性看待。

Around the world, only a few countries have legalized the practice of euthanasia, and the number of cases treated with euthanasia is growing in these countries at a slow pace. Why only such a few countries have passed the law for legalizing euthanasia? Many objecting opinions are voiced from the religious communities, arguing that only God should be in possession of such granting power in deciding the life span of individuals. However, I disagree with such reasoning because I do believe in one's right to decide when to eternally leave the world under certain circumstances, and will explain more in the following paragraph.

在全世界各地，只有幾個國家已經將安樂死合法化，而在這些國家中，實際實施安樂死的個案也是緩慢地成長，而為什麼這麼少的國家願意將安樂死合法化呢？其中一個原因是因為許多宗教團體持反對意見，認為只有上帝能夠有權決定每個人的生命多常，然而，我並不認同宗教團體的論點，而在某些特定情況下，支持個人安樂死的權益，且會在下一段詳述原因。

I support for individuals' right to legally undergo euthanasia under dire conditions, especially in terms of one's health issues. Take Taiwan for example, there are many instances where many patients are clinically sustained with all kinds of medical instruments but without prospect of recovery in the near future. For one, these sustained patients themselves oftentimes express no desire of prolonging their lives that way, and for another, these accumulated medical expenses are endured by the rest of the family, who not only exhaust much money but also physical and mental strength on such sustaining. In these kinds of cases, I think euthanasia should be legalized as there is literally no point of sustaining a body who only performs the most basic bodily functions, such as breathing, absorbing fluid foods, etc.

　　在某些特定健康方面的條件下，我支持個體應有法律保障，有權決定是否要對自身實施安樂死，就以台灣來說，有許多的案例為病患只能倚靠各種醫療器材來苟延壽命，但在長遠的未來中，卻無法實際地復原、恢復，對於病患本身來說，他們多半表示無意願以這種方式延長壽命，而對於病患家屬來說，他們也必須承受累積昂貴的醫療費用，也必須花費許多體力、精力，因此，在這種情況下，我贊同安樂死的合法化，因為若只是純粹用器材延長壽命，讓病患只是純粹施行最基本的生理功能，如呼吸、吸收流質食物等，是沒有意義的。

In general, I support euthanasia when patients are in such an irrecoverable state and agree to stop fighting for survival. After all, this is a natural process, and part of the circle of life.

總的來說，當病患處於無法復原、醫療的狀態，且同意死亡，我支持其安樂死的權益，畢竟，死亡只是自然的過程，也只是「有生必有死」循環的一部分。

6 性別平等
A can hold a candle to B 分庭抗禮

成語閱讀故事

　　成語「分庭抗禮」，其原出處來自《莊子‧漁父》中的「萬乘之主，千乘之君，見夫子未嘗不分庭抗禮。」，其所形容的意思即為兩方相對等，沒有優劣地位的區別，是處於同樣平等、對等的關係；在英文中，有句諺語可用來形容類似的概念，那就是「A can hold a candle to B」，形容 A 可以與 B 在實力、地位等不同條件下相抗衡，兩方是處於平等的狀態，而否定用法「A can't hold a candle to B」也很常在日常生活中聽到，指的即是 A 並無法與 B 相抗衡，且差距甚大。

寫作題目

Over the progression of society, gender issues have come a long way. Once upon a time, gender equality is such an obscure concept that it is not easily fathomable for many people, inclusive of some females themselves.

But now, society has come such a long way when it comes to protecting women's right at work. Mostly, the prevention of sexism is taken quite seriously throughout developed countries.

Now in today's world, the factor of "New Genders" (such as the LGBT community) comes into play, and ask for the same equal rights as the way male and female are both legally protected.

What is your view on this issue? Please explain.

寫作技巧解析

　　題目首先提到，在女權運動發跡的年代，人們還不能夠很輕易地接受兩性平權的觀念，主要是受到了傳統觀念的束縛，然而在現今已開發社會，兩性平權已成為非常基本的觀念，隨著時代的演變，也出現了所謂的「新性別」、LGBT 社群，這些個體也如之前追求兩性平權的先鋒，爭取他們應擁有的平等權利；以下範文採取支持立場，並舉例在各個不同的領域，「LGBT 總有傑出的代表能與傳統兩性分庭抗禮 Representatives of the LGBT community can hold a candle to representatives of the traditionally defined binary sex group」。

應試撇步

　　範文首段提到傳統的性別平等，在性別的區分上，是很「清楚界分的 clear-cut」。這種不容許灰色地帶的分法，只將性別區分為「二元的 binary」的男性與女性；然而，隨著時代的演進，應將「較狹隘的 narrower」的性別定義擴張，將 LGBT 社群「納入、包含 inclusive of」性別平等的訴求上，而文中也以「公開出櫃 openly gay」的奧運數度游泳冠軍伊恩‧索普為例，說明 LGBT 社群在許多方面就跟傳統男性女性一樣，應獲得同樣權益。

 作文範例　　🎧 MP3 024

With the progression of time, gender equality has taken up a new kind of meaning, not just as clear-cut as it used to be. In the early development of feminism, gender equality is simply an issue of equal rights between men and women. But now, as the society is becoming more open-minded, there are new additions to the traditionally accepted and defined binary sex group. Some of these so-called "New Genders" are members of the LGBT community. I personally support for equal rights for the community, and will explain why in the following paragraph.

　　隨著時代的演進，性別平等延伸至另一層的涵義，而非如以往的時代，將性別如此單純、清楚地以男性及女性來定義，就如當女性主義剛開始萌芽時，性別平等也單就以男性、女性之間的平權來探討，而發展至今日，社會也越趨開放，對於社會上原本所接受的二元男女性別分法，也有了新的發展，而這其中即包含了 LGBT 社群的成員；我個人對於 LGBT 社群爭取平權，抱持著支持的態度，原因會於下段詳述。

In many areas of life, there are quite a few illustrious representations on behalf of the LGBT community such as Ian Thorpe and others. Ian Thorpe now is an openly gay athlete who has won numerous Olympic swimming champion titles. This example illustrates the fact that, in many ways, representatives of the LGBT community can hold a candle to representatives of the traditionally defined sexes: male and female. We only need to think about the potential loss if we do not provide people like Ian get deserved equal rights. They might not have the chance to excel at what they do if they are discriminated against by the law or are treated unfairly by the society, and that would be a shame for societies to lose the honor brought upon by life champions like Ian Thorpe.

在人生中的各個領域,有許多代表 LGBT 社群的榮耀人物,舉例來說,在奧運比賽數度奪冠的游泳選手伊恩‧索普,即是個公開承認自己性傾向的選手,而伊恩的例子也證明了 LGBT 的社群代表,在許多方面是能夠與傳統二元男女性別分法的代表一樣優秀、分庭抗禮的,因此,若 LGBT 社群無法享有應有的平等權益,而無法培育、訓練出如伊恩般優秀的選手時,其對於社會及國家的損失將可想而知,因為他們若被法律歧視、或是被社會不合理對待,將可能無法在其專業領域中表現傑出,而社會及國家因而失去如伊恩般優秀的冠軍選手是很可惜的。

All in all, it is a great achievement for the early pioneers who have championed for gender equality, although in a narrower sense of equality between binary genders, that today's society does try to maintain and promote woman's rights. Now equality should be expanded to the broader sense of gender, one that is inclusive of the LGBT community.

　　總的來説，對於早期提倡二元兩性平權的先進來説，如今社會盡力維護、提倡女性權益的現象是個偉大的成就，而現在應秉持著同樣的精神，將性別平等的議題擴大，並將 LGBT 社群納入維護平等權益的對象。

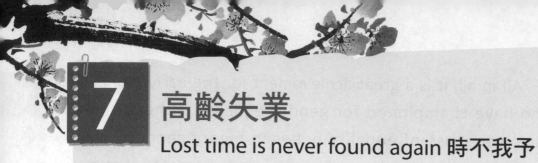

7 高齡失業

Lost time is never found again 時不我予

成語閱讀故事

　　成語「時不我予」所形容的是某人感嘆時間以及歲月的流失，但當初並沒有善加把握住機會，因而感嘆時機流逝、能改變的機會已失去，其出處來自《論語・陽貨》中所説的「日月逝矣，歲不我與。」；在英文中，有句經典名言「Lost time is never found again」，其所傳達對於時間流逝的感嘆，以及對於機會逝去的醒悟、認清，與「時不我予」的意涵相似，儘管兩句諺語皆傳達出對於失去、無法改變的感嘆，但某種程度上也傳達出一種已看開、豁達的意境。

寫作題目

The movie "The Intern" depicts the story of one certain retiree being too bored with retirement, and then goes to intern for one young start-up company.

The story is a positive one where the retiree proves his life-long experiences are very much valuable, although may stereotypically be deemed old-school by the younger generations or the general job market.

However, what if someone is unexpectedly forced out of employment at a relatively older age?

It does happen to some people who have not successfully saved enough retirement funds and not yet reached the age for retiring, but is let go from a company.

Do you think they still have a shot at that point? Please share your views.

寫作技巧解析

　　題目率先提到電影《高年級實習生》，說其內容描繪的是主角退休後不甘寂寞、因而返回職場的故事，雖然一開始工作職場並不看好他，因為高齡而不被重視，但最後主角證明薑還是老的辣，一生的經歷還是非常寶貴、值得重視的；以下範文採支持立場，認為活到老學到老，儘管高齡失業，儘管「時不我予 Lost time is never found again」，還是要堅定意志，累積的人生經驗，翻轉處境。

應試撇步

　　範文首段提到，「臨時、意外被裁員 unexpectedly laid off」的高齡員工，面對就業市場激烈的競爭及一般社會對於高齡失業的「刻板印象 stereotype」，造就了籠罩高齡失業的「悲觀的氛圍 pessimistic atmosphere」；第二段提到高齡失業的員工歷經較多人生的風雨及「起伏 ups and downs」，因此對於職場上各種人際間的關係，更能掌握、應對，之後也提到，調整心態來提高生產力，而不是「將思緒陷在過去流逝的時光 mull over the lost time」，是有機會化解危機的。

（高齢失業——Lost time is never found again）

作文範例　　　　　　　　　　　🎧 MP3 025

1 教育

2 社會法律議題

3 民生生活

In today's economic climate, it is common to find people who are suddenly forced out of employment. What happens when workers who are unexpectedly laid off are in a relatively older age group? With the job market being competitive everywhere and unshakable stereotypes of older people being let go of employment, the prospect of unemployed workers at older ages is grim. Nevertheless, I do not encourage people to participate in such a pessimistic atmosphere if they do find themselves in such a difficult situation, and will explain why in the following.

在今日此種的經濟環境，被臨時解雇的工作人員並不罕見，但高齡失業的員工該怎麼自我面對、調適呢？尤其在今日競爭激烈的職場，以及社會對於高齡失業員工的刻板印象，他們未來的前景更是慘淡，然而，我並不鼓勵在此困境的高齡失業員工沉溺於這種悲觀的氛圍，並會於下解釋原因。

For starters, people of relatively older ages have for sure lived a longer life, have gone through more ups and downs of what life brings. As a result, they have much more life experiences, which they can easily draw upon, for all different kinds of work situations. Oftentimes at the work place, knowing how to deal with people is even more important than one's specialized skills. Also, do not forget that every challenge is an opportunity, and despite the fact that it will be exceptionally challenging for people of middle ages to switch careers, it is not entirely impossible. As the saying goes, "Lost time is never found again." It would be much more productive to keep learning new skills to prove one's value for prospective employers, than to keep mulling over the lost time.

首先，高齡失業的族群，因為人生也走了大半部分，因此也經歷了較多的人生起伏，而也因為如此，他們能藉由自身的經驗，於工作職場上應對自如，而這些技能是很重要的，因為在職場上，很多時候與人相處的學問比個人的專業技能還要來得重要；另外，別忘了，每個挑戰的背後都是另一個機會，儘管對於中年失業、轉業的員工來說，挑戰縱然極困難，但也不是完全沒有機會，正如成語「時不我予」所傳達的，在當下來看，往日的時間、機會已過，然而應盡快調整心態，將注意力集中在新技能的學習，而不是沉溺在過去，才是有生產力的。

In conclusion, I think it is definitely possible for people who are laid off at an older age to turn a new leaf over their lives, and thrive on the new opportunity that is disguised in their current challenges.

總結來說，我認為對於高齡失業的人來說，要展開新的人生扉頁是絕對有可能的，甚至能夠在這被挑戰掩蓋的機會中，更加進一步發展、提昇。

8 賦稅
nibble away at something 蠶食鯨吞

📖 成語閱讀故事

　　成語「蠶食鯨吞」，其出處來自《韓非子‧存韓》中的「諸侯可蠶食而盡，趙氏可得與敵矣。」，其原本所形容的是用盡各種方法來侵略、掠奪別的國家的領地，不論是如桑蠶般慢慢地啃食桑葉，還是如深海中鯨魚般張口大吞，就是用盡各種方式來達成掠奪的目的；在英文中，常用「nibble away at something」這句話來形容某人不擇手段地來掠奪、佔盡他人的資源、財產，與「蠶食鯨吞」的意思相似，換句話說，也就是形容某人貪得無厭的意思。

寫作題目

In many parts of the world, how taxes are calculated is often critically scrutinized by both the tax payers and collectors.

Take the property tax in Taiwan for example, with the living expenses increasing on an annual basis and property prices skyrocketing through the roof, the government wishes to curtail market manipulation by property developers through a more stringent employment of property tax.

Through the amendments to property tax, the government aims to give a fairer right to people wishing to acquire a house of their own.

How do you think about this tactic as an attempt to curtail runaway property prices?

Do you agree with such a policy? Please explain your stance.

➕ 寫作技巧解析

　　題目提到，在全球許多地方，個人及企業稅的計算方式總是容易成為許多繳稅人、收稅機關的注目焦點，而以台灣的房屋稅為例，政府試圖以較嚴苛的房屋稅法來杜絕、制壓被房地產商炒房的高漲房價；以下範文採取支持的觀點，認為政府必須採取行動，如改革後的新制房屋稅，才較能制壓貪商「蠶食鯨吞」的炒房作為，面對「property developers nibble away at the monetary resources」的局面。

⑥ 應試撇步

　　範文提到，由於欠缺政府權威所訂定的相關法規、措施，台灣的房地產價格因為炒房而「失控 gone wild」，而政府打算藉由較「嚴峻的 stringent」賦稅措施，來「適度調節 moderately adjust」台灣的房地產市場，尤其當房地產商激進、「魯莽地 recklessly」賺取利潤，導致「資本主義扭曲、變形 capitalism gone awry」的現象時，政府更應當積極「介入 step in」，來協調、排解不公的現象。

作文範例

 MP3 026

In Taiwan, there are not proper regulations in place for the real estate market. As a result, the real estate prices are disproportionately higher than many other parts of the world. This phenomenon comes with a myriad of social issues, such as the injustice of living, younger generations not being able to afford a house of their own and so on. In order to weed out such problems one step at a time, the Taiwanese government is implementing stringent amendments to the originally existing property tax laws, hoping to gain back control over the gone-wild market of commercial real estates. I am personally in favor of such practice, and will further elaborate on my stance in the following.

　　在台灣，因為缺乏政府權威有效的控制手段，房地產價格被哄抬、失控，而也因為這個現象，帶來了許多社會問題，如居住正義、年輕世代買不起房子等議題，所以，台灣政府為了一一摒除這些問題，將實施較嚴峻的房屋稅改革，以期能夠協調已失控的房地產價格，而我個人支持政府的這些舉動、措施，且會在下段詳加說明。

To begin with, it is just a sooner-or-later matter for governments to take actions against such as runaway property prices in Taiwan. For many property developers, they would go through the lengths to where the money is, as they would love to nibble away at all the available monetary resources. On some level, it is understandable that people go after where the money is to be independently sufficient, but it would be a different story if they do so in a reckless manner and have no concern for other people being affected by these reckless behaviors. It is not socially responsible, and it is essentially capitalism gone awry. Therefore, we need government to step in, and gain back control through the revision of tax laws.

首先，台灣政府對於失控的房價採取相關應對措施只是遲早的問題，對於許多房地產商來說，他們的目標是將利潤最大化、蠶食鯨吞地將可賺取的利益到手，而儘管在某一層面上來說，企業賺取利益原本就是他們應有的權益，但當他們不擇手段，並對於被其行為所影響的其它人毫無同理心時，就是個不一樣的狀況了，這不僅對於整個社會來說是毫無責任感的，且是個資本主義扭曲、變形的經典例子，所以，政府的確應當出手，藉由稅賦來適當調整失控的狀況。

To summarize, I stand in favor of the Taiwanese government's implementation of reformed property tax laws as an attempt to moderately adjust the commercial real estate market to a more reasoned condition. After all, it is the government's responsibility to step in when capitalism has morphed into a morbid, unfair state.

總結來說，我支持政府藉由房屋稅改革來試圖調整房地產市場的狀況，畢竟當資本主義已發展至病態、不公的局面時，政府的責任原本就是應適度地介入、調整，排解不公的現象。

1 教育

2 社會法律議題

3 民生生活

9 城鄉差距
The sky's the limit 人往高處去，水往低處流

📖 成語閱讀故事

　　諺語「人往高處去，水往低處流」，所講的是人應當積極鞭策、激勵自己，藉由努力來提昇自己的水平、水準，不論是物質的客觀因素，或是所處環境等外在因素，還是內在的知識、觀念等內涵的昇華、提昇，都是身為人所應該追求的目標，而不是像水流般越往低處流，而墮落成習，使個人的格局、水準降低；在英文中，可用「The sky's the limit」來形容類似的概念，其所指的是若任何人有任何的目標、理想，都應當努力去執行，因為人的潛力無限，任何事都有可能達成，因為最遠的天空才是極限，而其背後的意涵與諺語「人往高處去，水往低處流」是一樣的。

Across the globe, the difference of development between rural and urban areas is getting more and more pronounced. In Taiwan, the three major cities are located respectively at the northern, central, and southern part of the island country, and areas beyond the scope of these three major urban areas are faced with relatively limited resources from the central government, problems of not too many job opportunities and so on.

As a result, younger generations move from areas that are not as developed to the major cities, attempting to capitalize on the many opportunities and resources offered by such kind of a metropolis.

But in recent years, there seems to be a reverse trend where some of the younger generations of Taiwan are returning to their hometowns to contribute to local economic growth.

What is your take on this? Please explain.

寫作技巧解析

　　題目問道，當隨著世界各地的城鄉差距發展越來越大時，年輕世代族群總是離鄉背井，為了追求更好、更進步的生活，前往大都市找尋機會，以實踐理想。然而，最近幾年來，有趨勢顯示台灣的某些年輕人願意回到家鄉，雖不像大都市般充滿機會，但願意在家鄉協助創造機會，以利發展；以下範文採取支持立場，認為儘管「人往高處去，水往低處流 The sky's the limit」的觀念還是盛行，但年輕人願意回家鄉創造機會、打拼，也是很值得鼓勵的。

應試撇步

　　文章開門見山提到「人往高處去，水往低處流 The sky's the limit」，並且解釋說，這也就是為什麼許多年輕人「直覺地 instinctively」畢業後選擇到大城市打拼，「實踐理想 fulfill their aspirations」，然而，隨著城市發展的「成熟化 maturation」，年輕人在大城市實踐理想的機會「正在漸少 slimming down」，而隨著網際網路以及科技的發展，年輕人回到家鄉另開局面、打拼的方案，其時機實在是再適合不過了。

 作文範例

As the saying goes, "The sky's the limit," and that is why youngsters, when they first come upon entering the workforce after graduation, tend to instinctively migrate to big cities from their hometowns in search of better job opportunities that fulfill their aspirations. However, over the recent years with the progression in technology and the congestion of urban areas, some youngsters are choosing a different route. They are going back to their hometowns to realize what they want out of their life. In my opinion, I champion such a phenomenon and will explain further in the following.

正如諺語「人往高處去，水往低處流」所形容的，人應當努力往更好的生活邁進，也正因如此，許多社會新鮮人在一畢業後，即從家鄉前往大城市找尋更好的機會，以求實現自己對於人生的期許，然而，最近幾年由於科技進步，以及城市的成熟化、雍塞等現象，有些年輕人反而選擇反其道而行，選擇回到自己的家鄉來實現理想，而在我看來，我支持、提倡這股逆潮流，並會於下段解釋原因。

First of all, as cities around the world are becoming ever more developed, they are also congested with a constant inflow of workers trying to make a living and create a life of their own in these so-called "promise lands." In other words, along with such urban maturation on city development, opportunities can be slimming down for new generations trying to make it in a big city. In addition, there are other issues regarding such maturation, take the high living expenses incurred in big cities for example. Therefore, it would make sense for younger generations to look for the alternative to realize their life vision and goals. Besides, with today's technological advancement, returning back to hometowns can be a great idea.

首先，當世界各地的城市越來越進步發展時，這些城市也因為尋找工作的人不間斷地湧入，而越加壅塞，只因他們想在所謂的「夢想之地」生存、創造屬於自己的生活，換句話說，當城市發展已到如此成熟化的階段，對於想在大城市實踐夢想的年輕人來說，機會將越來越渺茫，而這種城市發展的成熟化，也帶來了其它議題，如城市生活的高開銷等等，所以，對於年輕人來說，尋找代替城市打拼的替代方案來實踐人生理想與目標，是很合理的，並且加上現今科技的發達，回到家鄉打拼儼然是個不錯的選項。

In conclusion, as long as younger generations get to know how to effectively utilize the Internet to their best advantage, it does not really matter if they are making money in big cities or not. Besides, it would definitely help boost the local economy if youngsters decide to stay where they are originally from and work hard.

　　總結來說，只要年輕世代瞭解如何有效地運用網路資源，其是否身處在大城市工作並不會有太大的影響，而且，他們若回到家鄉打拼，必定能夠促進、幫助當地的經濟發展，是件好的事情。

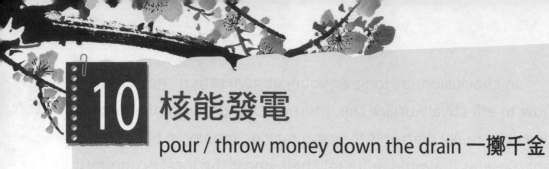

10 核能發電
pour / throw money down the drain 一擲千金

成語閱讀故事

　　成語「一擲千金」，其所形容的是某人對於金錢的花費毫不在乎，在金錢的使用上沒有限度，能夠承受一次性的大筆消費，其出處來自唐朝作家吳象所著《少年行》中的文句「一擲千金渾是膽，家無四壁不知貧」，常用在博弈遊戲的場合中，形容賭客下注時的大膽、闊氣；而在英文中，可用「pour / throw money down the drain」來形容相似的行為，指某人對於錢的態度不甚在乎，猶如是將身邊的錢財丟入、沖下水槽管線，一去無蹤了。

In Taiwan, there were heated discussions surrounding the issue of whether it is a good idea to build the fourth nuclear power plant.

On one hand, proponents of the construction argue that the fourth plant can bring an abundant flow of low-cost electricity supplies in the future.

On the other hand, opponents argue that for a small country like Taiwan, in terms of its geological size, how the government who intends to deal with the resulting nuclear wastes can bring potential hazards to the country.

Do you support the construction of additional nuclear power plants in Taiwan? Please provide your reasoning behind your stance.

寫作技巧解析

　　題目提到，有關台灣核能發電廠興建的議題，支持者認為應當興建，因為核能發電廠能夠帶來充沛及廉價的供電，但另一方面，反對興建的聲浪認為，以台灣相對人口稠密、面積小的國家來說，核能發電廠所產生的核廢料處理有可能會對台灣社會造成危害，而以下範文採反對興建的立場，並說明政府興建的花費有如「一擲千金 pour / throw money down the drain」，應當慎思。

應試撇步

　　範文說道，有關「核能發電廠 nuclear power plant」的興建，支持與反對的聲浪各有論述，但若政府無法以公平、妥善的方式，來處理所衍生的「放射性物質 radioactive materials」的話，應當朝向開發「綠能源 green energy」及「再生能源 sustainable energy」等這方面的研究，因為儘管政府目前宣稱放置在蘭嶼的核廢料有採取封閉、保護等措施，但還是無法切確、果斷地提供證明，來保證此種的處置方式不會對居民健康產生「隱伏的 insidious 的危害。

 作文範例　　　　　　　　　　🔊 MP3 028

In Taiwan, the issue of whether or not an additional nuclear power plant shall be granted construction permission is much debated. For backers of the construction plan, they feel a nuclear power plant brings a steady flow of supplied electricity at a low cost, and thus able to cast a lesser burden on citizens as far as living expenses are concerned. On the contrary, for people who are against the construction, they feel that it is unscrupulous for the government to start building a new plant when there are no fair solutions, at the moment, for the disposal of nuclear wastes.

在台灣，有關是否應允許新的核能發電廠的興建是個棘手的議題，對於支持興建的人來說，核能發電廠能夠帶來穩定、低廉的供電，也因此能夠讓人民減少民生開銷的負擔，相反地，對於反對者來說，他們認為在現今尚未有公平、公正來處理核廢料方法的當下，再度興建新的核能發電廠是個莽撞的舉動。

To begin with, the current solution taken by the Taiwanese government to deal with the derivative nuclear wastes is to ship them to the island of Lanyu. Although the government does release a statement ensuring that these radioactive materials are properly enclosed to prevent Lanyu inhabitants from being hazardously affected, there is no certain way to conclude that their health is not impacted in an insidious way. Secondly, the cost of building a nuclear power plant is substantial. The government should be exploring the possibility of greener, more sustainable energy sources before throwing money down the drain on building another plant.

　　首先，目前台灣政府面對核能發電廠所衍生的核廢料議題，其措施為將其安排運送至蘭嶼放置，儘管政府已發佈公告，說明類似核廢料這種具放射性的物質，其本身密封的處理方式能夠避免蘭嶼居民的健康受到侵害，但還是無法確切、有效地證明這些居民不會在時間的累積下，健康受到影響；第二，核能發電廠的建蓋需要一筆可觀的花費，因此，政府在預算花費上一擲千金前，應當多方評估綠能源、再生能源的方案。

All in all, I oppose the reckless momentum of continual addition of a nuclear power plant to the existing ones in Taiwan. As explained above, until a fairer, more proper way of handling nuclear wastes is proposed, the government should gear towards unlocking the potential of what sustainable energy can bring in the long run.

總而言之，我反對在台灣持續擴建核能發電廠的主張，因為如上所述，當如何更公平、妥善地來處理核廢料的問題無法被有效解決時，政府應當先將精力轉向瞭解如何開發再生能源的潛能，以利長久的未來發展。

1 教育

2 社會法律議題

3 民生生活

11 居住正義

The rich get richer, the poor go hungry 朱門酒肉臭，路有凍死骨

成語閱讀故事

　　諺語「朱門酒肉臭，路有凍死骨」，所形容的是社會中有財有勢的人家，能夠富裕到儲藏過多的食材、酒肉，而導致有吃不完、放到腐臭的現象，但另一方面，路邊卻有窮困的人，因為連最基本的吃穿溫飽都無法滿足而凍死街頭，感嘆社會中現實、極度不公的現象，其出自唐朝詩人杜甫的《自京赴奉先詠懷五百字》中的名言詩句；在英文中，常聽到「The rich get richer, the poor go hungry」，其所指的即是此種社會財富分配不均、不公的現象，道出有錢人越加有錢，而家境貧困的人連生活溫飽都面臨困難。

In Taipei, the property prices have been soaring through the roof to the point where most average people would have never been able to afford a house on their own.

This is especially true when their finance for purchasing a house is purely made up of regular paychecks. Instead, properties are being sold to people who are wealthy enough to acquire them mainly for the purpose of investments.

Many argue that such a phenomenon has left the average people hanging, with no feasible means of coming up with sufficient funds to cut a deal in today's astronomically-priced real estate market.

One method to counteract such inequality of living between the rich and the poor, the government proposed the development of social housing. Do you agree with such a policy vision?

寫作技巧解析

題目提到，台北的房屋價格已高漲到一般人無法負擔的程度，而當購買房屋的資金來源純粹來自個人工作的固定薪水時，其無法負擔的程度更是如此，而政府解決的辦法之一為建立、推廣社會住宅；以下範文採取支持社會住宅的立場，認為政府應當積極推廣社會住宅，抑止「朱門酒肉臭，路有凍死骨 The rich get richer, the poor go hungry」的社會不公現象。

應試撇步

範文提到，台北的房價飆漲，年輕世代難以籌備「足夠的 sufficient」的資金及貸款來購屋，而政府提供的其一解方為「社會住宅 social housing」，其試圖藉由社會住宅，來解決目前台北「失控的 runaway」的房價，並避免「被哄抬 inflated」的價格來加深富人與一般人間原本已存在的「不平等 inequity」，也因此本篇範文採取支持的立場，鼓勵政府推行社會住宅的措施。

 作文範例　　　　　　　　　　　　　　⊙ MP3 029

In Taipei, younger generations are having a hard time preparing funds and coming up with sufficient payment plans to meet today's runaway property prices. The seed of this phenomenon is planted by a lack of governmental control in place and the development of market capitalism that has been much charged with greed and exploitation. Fortunately, despite the fact that the development of this city has been afflicted by this conundrum for years, the government is now taking actions against inflated prices that are instrumental in further enabling the inequity between the rich and the poor.

在台北，年輕世代難以準備出足夠的資金及付款計畫來面對今日失控、高漲的房屋單價，而問題的根源除了政府缺乏相關管控措施的原因外，市場資本主義在貪婪及剝削心態的發展下，也成了助因。幸運地是，儘管台北這個城市的整體發展，多年來因為這個難題，而受到阻礙、束縛，政府已開始展現決意，來面對、處理這種更加深貧富差距的房價哄抬現象。

One of the solutions proposed by the government is to make social housing more readily available to its citizens. Although there are certain rules and regulations imposed upon social housing applications, for many of the younger generations, the social housing program provides them with a better chance of having a place to call their own, albeit the fact that social housing cannot be permanently owned but is rather dealt with on lease terms. Hence, I support the attention that the development of social housing programs are receiving, because the more attention and funds are allocated towards the programs' development, the more chance that citizens can enjoy what is essentially a basic human right, which is the right to have a house of their own, not the one that parents kindly share with their adult children.

政府所提出的其中一個解方為社會住宅的推廣方案，讓其能夠造福更多的市民。而儘管社會住宅的申請有相關的法律及規定，但對於年輕世代的許多人來說，社會住宅提供他們一個能夠擁有屬於自己住所的機會，儘管社會住宅的永久所有權並不能夠被購得，而只能以租用的方式使用；因此，我支持政府開始著重社會住宅發展的態度，並支持其將注意力及資金分配到社會住宅方案，因為分配越多，市民越有機會能夠享有基本人權，能夠擁有一個自己的住宅，而能避免勞煩父母、與他們同住。

All in all, I support the government's effort to promote social housing. Otherwise, the phenomenon of what is described as "The rich get richer, the poor go hungry" will only be getting worse, not able to improve life quality for ordinary citizens.

總結來說，我支持政府發展社會住宅的努力、付出，否則這種「朱門酒肉臭，路有凍死骨」的社會現象只會越加嚴重，無法提升一般市民的生活品質。

12 勞動權益

someone is out of touch with reality 何不食肉糜

成語「何不食肉糜」是用來指管理者無法深刻瞭解民間疾苦，而無法以有效的策略、對策來處理問題，其出處來自《晉書‧惠帝記》中，提到當出現「天下荒亂，百姓餓死」的情事時，晉惠帝回應：「何不食肉糜？」，也就是在詢問說，百姓們為什麼不吃肉粥來填飽肚子就好了呢？由此回應，晉惠帝與民間百姓生活脫節的程度，可見一斑；在英文中，可用「someone is out of touch with reality」來形容某人的行為舉止如晉惠帝一般，由於背景、生活優渥，而不知民間大眾的煩惱、掙扎。

寫作題目

In Taiwan, the working conditions and benefits are one of the worst amongst developed countries. Take starting salaries for example, the starting salaries that are legally allowed for a university graduate are NTD$22,000.

However, when further examined, Taiwan boasts of one of the most highly-educated society population, churning out a constant flow of postgraduates and college graduates into the job market on a yearly basis.

The low salary and working environment that encourages overtime working pose a serious threat to the balance of the Taiwanese job market.

What is your take on this issue? Please explain.

寫作技巧解析

　　題目提到，台灣的工作環境，與許多已開發的國家相比，還有許多進步的空間。舉例來說，台灣雖然擁有大量的高教育、知識份子，但談論到薪水的支付時，法定最低薪資卻只要符合新台幣兩萬兩千元的門檻即可；以下範文採取反對的立場，認為「某些政府官員、企業老闆何不食肉糜 the government officials and business owners are out of touch with reality」，不知民間疾苦，認為此等的法定薪水是合理的。

應試撇步

　　題目說道，台灣「法律規範、有效的 legally bound」的「最低薪資 minimum wage」為新台幣兩萬兩千元，而這種薪資在扣除「日常生活開銷 daily living expenses」後，幾近被「沖銷 offset」而難以積蓄，而此種社會狀況容易使員工「心生不滿 disgruntled」，而若要改善此種狀況，政府官員及企業老闆必須率先瞭解，若能夠合理地提升薪資水準，將創造「雙贏的 mutually beneficial」的局面。

作文範例　　　　　　　　　　　　　　🔘 MP3 030

1 教育

2 社會法律議題

3 民生生活

In Taiwan, the minimum wages that are legally bound are set at the threshold of NTD$22,000. Some argue that this threshold not properly set as NTD$22,000 can hardly cover the daily living expenses for a fresh college graduate, especially those who migrate from other areas of Taiwan to the country's major cities. In fact, this amount of salary payment is so easily offset by earners' daily expenses that saving for the future becomes extremely difficult to do. Therefore, I do not support the current amount of NTD$22,000 as a minimum wage standard, and would further state the reasons behind my stance in the following.

在台灣，法定最低薪資的標準門檻為新台幣兩萬兩千元，而有些人認為，這最低薪資的法定門檻並不妥當，因為這樣的薪資對於大學剛畢業的社會新鮮人來說，用來支付日常生活的開銷已有一些困難，更別說是從別的縣市來到大都市中打拼的青年了，而事實上，由於此種薪資非常容易被日常的生活開銷打平，因此更別提積蓄的習慣了，所以，我並不支持目前法律所規定的最低薪資兩萬兩千元，且會於下段解釋原因。

For starters, the Taiwanese education system provides a yearly supply of highly-educated batch of postgraduates and college graduates into the workforce. When compared to other developed countries, Taiwan's starting salaries for fresh college graduates are much lower than those of their counterparts in those countries. As a result, higher education graduates are not receiving the kind of salary amount that is an adequate reflection of their educational background. This can further lead to disgruntled work force across the country, and as some management theory indicates, the lesser satisfactory the workforce is with their conditions, the lower productivity and work quality businesses are going to get out of those workers. Therefore, the government should consider reasonably raising the minimum standard upward to increase job satisfaction amongst workers.

首先，台灣的教育體制為台灣的就業市場，每年持續提供高教育程度的研究所、大學畢業生，然而，當與其它已開發國家相比，若以薪水來衡量，台灣對於剛大學畢業的社會新鮮人，其所給予的起薪相對低很多，換句話說，知識份子領取無法反映其價值的薪水，而這社會現象也導致員工對於雇主心生不滿，但正如某管理理論所言，若員工對於所出工作環境不滿，其生產力及工作品質也將相對地下降，因此，政府應當合理地調高最低法定薪資以提升其工作滿意度。

To conclude, when it comes to the issue of minimum wages, the government officials and business owners are out of touch with reality. To improve, they need to understand that it is mutually beneficial to increase one's salary amount.

總結來說，政府官員及企業老闆時常展現「何不食肉糜」、與現實脫節的心態，若想改善現今的社會現況，這些官員及老闆需充分瞭解，合理地提高薪資，將有助於創造雙贏的局面。

13 民主政治

too many cooks in the kitchen 人多嘴雜

成語閱讀故事

　　成語「人多嘴雜」所形容的是對於同一件事情，每個人都有屬於自己的見解、意見，因此在做決策時，反而會因為過多且分歧的建議，而無法有效地達成共識，將事情解決；在英文中，有句慣用語「too many cooks in the kitchen」來表達相同的概念，其字面上的意思是說，廚房裡有太多的廚師了，而每位廚師都有自己對於料理的見解，因此要達成共識並不是件簡單的事情，而有時也會聽到「too many cooks spoil the broth」，表示太多的廚師，反而「人多嘴雜」、無法煮出好湯頭。

 寫作題目

Democracy is something that has been fought for throughout human history, and is much enjoyed and celebrated in many parts of the world.

However, the degree of democracy is often the subject of discussion among scholars disputing over the right balance to strike in terms of how democratic a country is.

Some argue that too many opinions could lead to a potential stalemate on a lot of issues, while others think that people should all be given an opportunity to express how they feel about a certain subject, and should be able to resort to legal actions when they feel their rights are being violated.

What are your opinions on this? Please share and explain.

✚ 寫作技巧解析

　　題目說道，民主是絕大多數國家及社會人民所樂於享有的，然而，在各種社會議題上，一個民主政治的國家其民主、民意開放的程度扮演了重要的角色，因此民主政治及其程度上的拿捏，也是個值得探討的議題；以下範文採取反對民意過度開放的立場，認為在攸關社會國家福祉的議題上，有時應避免「人多嘴雜 too many cooks in the kitchen」的狀態，以免最後無法有效執行計畫、政策，「反倒 spoil the broth」。

◎ 應試撇步

　　範文提到，對於民主政治的發展，有些人認為「人多嘴雜」，容易「阻礙 impede」社會的快速發展，有些人則認為民主政治的價值應當是「不動搖的 unwavering」以及「永久的 ever-lasting」的基本人權，但當民主政治已發展至「偏離的 skewed」的價值觀，而不是原本以造福「全體社會福祉 the greater good」為理念時，政府應當試圖「達到適當的平衡 strike the right balance」，才能夠真正創造整體社會的進步才是。

 作文範例   🎵 MP3 031

As with many things in life, too much of something can sometimes work against what is originally intended for. Take democracy for example, it is one of the things that people and social activists would gladly utilize to achieve the greater good for societies. However, to what degree should democracy be promoted and allowed is oftentimes the topic of discussions among social commentators. Some fear that too many cooks in the kitchen could impede the society from moving forwards with efficiency. On the contrary, those who champion the virtues of democracy hold such a view that democracy should not be compromised in any sort of way. On this issue, I take the opposing stance to overly-developed democracy that has been skewed from the values' original intentions in increasing people's benefits.

正如生活中的許多事物，其過多的提供反而有時會有反效果，以民主政治為例，儘管大部份人民及社運人士樂於利用民主，來促成社會更加的福祉，然而，民主政治應當被給予、鼓勵的程度，時常是社會評論家的討論主題，有些人不願見到因人多嘴雜，而阻礙社會有效率地前進、進步的局面，但也有些人認為，民主政治所倡導的精神，應當是至死不渝的，且本當就該以基本人權的觀念來看待，不可妥協；對於這個議題，我反對過度發展的民主政治，尤其當它已背離原本所提倡的精神，而無法有效創造社會福祉時。

As previously stated, too many cooks in the kitchen, if not managed in an organized manner, can easily add more chaos into existing social issues that are already complex in nature. For instance, the issue of urban renewal is a great example showcasing the pros and cons of democracy that is overly developed. For the pros, individuals can have their opinions heard and rights maintained to the fullest if they are unwilling to budge in negotiations with the government. On the flip side of this is that the renewal process can take years if the government is too busy making every individual content with their remuneration. This is a classic example of government overly protecting citizen rights at the expense of realizing the greater good for society.

如以上所提到的，人多嘴雜容易礙事，尤其當以沒有條理的方式來處理時，將在原本複雜的社會議題上造成更多混亂，比方說，若以城市更新的議題來看，其展現了過度發展的民主政治帶來的優缺點。優點方面，民眾個人能夠有效表達自己的立場，且能在與政府的協商中，盡量維持自己的權益，但反方面來說，城市更新的效率將被拖累、延緩多年，因為政府忙於協商，忙著與民眾協調補償金等議題，而這正是政府過度保護民眾個人權益，忽略了整體社會福祉創造的典型例子。

In short, I oppose the over protection of individual rights that could only be realized at the expense of the fulfillment of the greater good. There should be a right amount of balance to strike, and that is where the government should aim at to more effectively bring about social and economic progression.

簡短來說，我反對政府對於民眾個人權益過度的保護，而犧牲了整體社會、民眾的福祉，反而，政府應當尋求平衡，以利社會、經濟能夠更有效地發展。

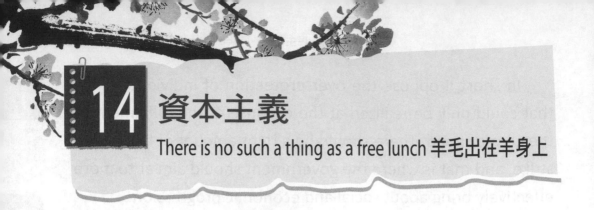

14 資本主義

There is no such a thing as a free lunch 羊毛出在羊身上

成語閱讀故事

　　諺語「羊毛出在羊身上」，其所指的是某人所獲取的利益，表面上看似賺到，但實際上其所獲取的利益，正是來自其個人的辛勞與付出所賺得的，簡單來說，就是在表面上給予勞動付出者好處，但事實上，這些好處早已計算在這些勞動者所付出的勞力代價內，而從某些角度來看，可說是對於勞動者某種程度的剝削；在英文中，有句慣用語「There is no such a thing as a free lunch.」，其所形容的，正是道出「羊毛出在羊身上」背後的真實面，不過這句英文慣用語帶有較正面的語調，鼓勵勞動、付出賺取成果，反觀「羊毛出在羊身上」帶有較負面的語調，揭露現代社會貿易、商業的黑暗面。

寫作題目

With the advent and development of capitalism, the global market is getting ever more competitive and intense. In turn, this increased competition leads to business decision-makers aggressively exploring ways to achieve profit maximization, and they find that international trade is one way to do so.

Many of these international conglomerates move production bases to countries where an abundant source of labor and lax regulations is provided.

Some argue that this is capitalism at its finest, as this practice is much capable of cutting costs, while others are afraid that this phenomenon is capitalism gone awry. What is your view on this? And why?

1 教育

2 社會法律議題

3 民生生活

寫作技巧解析

　　題目提到，隨著資本主義的誕生及發展，國際大企業努力實踐利潤最大化的願景，而其中一個方法，就是將生產、製造基地移至開發中國家，而得以享有充沛的廉價勞力及較鬆散的法規、法條，這樣能夠有效地降低成本，並將利益最大化；以下範文採反對立場，反對此種剝削的行為，並認為開發中國家的政府應當瞭解「羊毛出在羊身上 There is no such a thing as a free lunch.」，應想辦法折衷，以降低此剝削行為。

應試撇步

　　範文提到，隨著「科技的進步 technological advance」，國際貿易的發展「正值最佳時機 no greater time than now」，而當許多大企業將重點放在「利潤最大化 profit maximization」以及如何「降低成本 cut costs」時，這些企業自然將前往開發中國家來設置「生廠基地 production base」，以把握「廉價勞力 low-cost laborers」及「鬆散的 lax」的法規、法條，而其解決的辦法，則是當地政府應當「捍衛 safeguard」當地民眾的權益，以「杜絕 eradicate」國外大企業剝削的行為。

 作文範例

With the technological advances made in the last couple of years, there has been no greater time than now for the development of international trade. However, many business conglomerates are so focused on the realization of profit maximization that they jump at any chance to push down costs. One way they are able to achieve this is through taking advantage of sowing low-cost laborers that are found in developing countries. Another element that adds to the appeal of transferring production bases to the developing countries is the relatively lax laws and regulations in place. Pertinent laws and regulations governing working conditions for laborers, duties of being environmentally responsible, and so on, are not as stringent as those enforced in their counterpart developed countries.

隨著近幾年時代科技的進步，對於國際貿易的發展是再好不過的時機了，然而，當許多國際大企業將發展重心、重點著重在利潤最大化的目標時，他們願意把握任何機會，只為了來降低成本。而實現這個目標的其中一個方法，就是好好把握開發中國家的低成本勞力資源，另外，引誘這些大企業將生產基地轉移至開發中國家的其它誘因，包括了與已開發國家相比，相對鬆散的法律及規範，其中包含了管理勞工工作環境，以及企業的環保責任等相關的法規。

To this practice, I take the opposing stance, and do not support the intent behind these conglomerates who only plan to exploit resources but not intend to fairly reciprocate to those who grab resources from. Such practice is neither ethical nor socially responsible, and those who conduct such business operations purely for the purpose of profit maximization should be more closely regulated to safeguard the rights of the local people. The local governments should be aware of the fact that there is no such thing as a free lunch, and refrain themselves from blindly opening up opportunities for large businesses treating them unfairly.

　　對於這種作為，我抱持著反對的態度，並且不支持這些大企業背後欲剝削資源的意圖，但卻不願公平合理地對待、回饋受其影響的人民，這樣的作為不僅是不道德的，也是對其所影響的社會不負責任的行為，而純粹以利潤最大化為目標的企業，當地政府應當更加仔細地控管，以維護當地民眾的權益，且當地政府應當注意、認知羊毛出在羊身上的道理，而盡量避免盲目地開放當地的資源，讓大企業以不公平的方式對待當地的政府及民眾。

In conclusion, I do not encourage the exploitation of developing countries' workforce and natural resources. As the local governments can be easily blinded by gains in the near future, more international laws and regulations should be enacted to eradicate such unfair practices so that a more balanced development of the world can be made.

　　總結而論，我不鼓勵對於開發中國家的勞工及自然資源採取剝削的舉止，而當當地的政府容易短視近利時，應當訂定更多的國際法規及條款，才能杜絕不平等的開發，也才能朝向全球均衡的開發、進步邁進。

1 教育

2 社會法律議題

3 民生生活

15 環境保護
blaze a trail 披荊斬棘

📖 成語閱讀故事

　　成語「披荊斬棘」，其出處來自《後漢書・馮異傳》中「為吾披荊棘，定關中。」，其所形容的是在前往成功的路途上，儘管困難重重，但某人仍能夠堅定意志，不畏困難、挑戰，將過程中所遇到的各種阻礙，如蔓生的荊棘般一一鏟除；在英文中，有句類似的用語，那就是「blaze a trail」，其字面上是指「開發、開闢一條新的道路」，傳達出某人堅定、並不會輕易地因眼前的難題而氣餒的態度，而其所運用的意象與「披荊斬棘」雷同，皆是以樹林、道路為意象，來形容相同的事物，另外，「blaze a trail」在形容不畏艱難、一一排除困難的同時，也帶有先鋒創始、開拓的意涵。

寫作題目

With the development of global industries, advocates from developed countries are fighting to keep the environmental health at its best shape. During the Industrial Revolution, people were solely focused on expansion, growth, and other developments but unaware of the fact that what they were aggressively pursuing comes at the expense of the environment.

On the contrary, people of today are well aware of the detrimental impacts that any reckless industrial developments can bring onto the environment, and they are coming up with international laws and regulations to curb further environmental deterioration.

However, developing countries are opposing such restrictions, stating that developed countries already had their turn exploiting gains at the expense of the environment, and they should have the chance, too.

What is your take on this? Please explain.

寫作技巧解析

　　題目提到，隨著產業的發展，許多已開發國家聯合制定了相關的國際法律及法規，以保障地球環境的保存，儘管在 18、19 世紀發生工業革命時，當時對於環境保護的觀念尚未健全，所以當時西方國家的發展與擴張，皆不受現今所制定的法規所管，但也因此，現今的開發中國家抱有異議、認為不公平；以下範文採反對開發中國家抱有異議的立場，並用「披荊斬棘 blaze a trail」來形容這幾年已開發國家對環境保護所投注的心力及努力，並認為全球皆應當遵守才是。

應試撇步

　　範文提到，科學研究顯示，環境被工業的擴張「負面、不利地影響 adversely affected」，比如說「氣候變遷 climate change」以及「海平面上升 rising sea levels」，也因此，國際環保法規的建立就是為了要更有效地來控管「汙染源 pollutants」，讓企業營運所創造的汙染能夠「降到最低 keep to the minimum」，而儘管開發中國家對於這些國際法條抱持著「異議 dissent」，但若遵循這些法規，「最終的受益者 the ultimate beneficiary」也將會是他們自己。

作文範例

    With scientific evidence showing that the environment has been adversely affected by the industrial expansion, notably during the Industrial Revolution periods, developed countries that have kept a close eye on environmental issues, such as climate change, rising sea levels, and so on, are coming up with ways to regulate industrial practices. Thus, international laws and regulations aimed for the aid of better management on environmental pollutants are created. Nevertheless, what is interesting is the dissent coming from today's developing counties, voicing opinions that these laws and regulations are hypocritical as developed countries had already had the chance at reckless expansion. Developing countries feel unfairly treated as they would face more roadblocks on the way to prosperity.

    隨著科學的進展，許多研究結果顯示產業的擴張對於環境有著負面、不利的影響，尤其是在工業革命時期所造成的影響甚鉅，所以對於環境議題，如氣候變遷、海平面上升等議題有持續關注的已開發國家，開始找尋方法來管控工商業的發展及作為，也因此有國際法律及法規的誕生、發展，而其目的是來幫助對於環境污染因子的控管；然而，有趣的是，今日的發開中國家對於環境保護法條的制定帶有異議，認為這些法條是虛偽的，因為這些已開發國家之前早已有了無後顧之憂、全力發展的機會，而現在制定這些法條，將使開發中國家在達到繁榮的發展程度上，面臨更多阻礙，而認為這

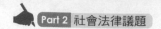

是不公平的待遇。

My personal view is that I do not concur with such contention. First of all, today's business climate is much different from the one in the past, certainly not the least different than the one during the Industrial Revolution. Today businesses are blessed with the convenience of modern technology, and with that convenience, keeping the pollution of business operations to the minimum is not too much of an outrageous request by all means. What's more, with the developed countries having blazed a trail for environmental protection, developed countries should take advantage of existing laws and regulations as they are ultimately protecting their own natural resources and environment.

以我個人的觀點來說，我並不支持開發中國家的論述；首先，今日的商業環境與過去的環境差距甚大，尤其是在工業革命時期的商業環境，更是完全不一樣的，像今日的企業可享有現代科技帶來的便利，而這些便利，對於企業將汙染源降到最低，從任何角度來看，並不會是件很不合理的要求，而且，既然已開發國家已披荊斬棘，克服重重困難建立起環境保護的法規，開發中國家應當好好利用現行法規，畢竟他們最終保護的還是屬於他們自己的自然資源、環境。

In summary, I do not support developing countries' dissent because the business environment has changed radically since the Industrial Revolution. Secondly, by obeying the international laws and regulations for environmental protection, developing countries are the ones who would eventually hold control over the protected natural resources; in other words, the ultimate beneficiary in the scenario.

總結概述，我不支持開發中國家的反對聲浪，因為自從工業革命後，商業環境已大幅改變，第二，換句話說，遵守國際環保法規的行為，最終受益者將會是開發中國家的政府及人民，因為他們最終還是擁有被保護的自然資源、環境，而可善加利用。

part **3** / 民生
生活

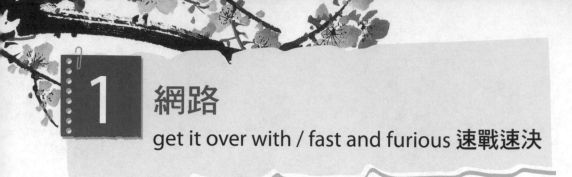

1 網路
get it over with / fast and furious 速戰速決

📖 成語閱讀故事

　　成語「速戰速決」，所形容的是某人用有效率、快速的方法來完成某個任務，一點都不拖泥帶水，也帶有著不期望將某事延長，只希望能夠快速解決的心態；在英文中，可常常聽到某人說道：「get it over with」，其所傳達的，正是「速戰速決」背後的心態，不拖拉，只想有效率、快速地來解決身邊的瑣事；另外，由於電影「玩命關頭 Fast and Furious」的賣座及成功，現代英語中也可經常聽到「fast and furious」這句話，來形容某人或某事正瘋狂、快速地進行，而其也帶有著「速戰速決」的概念。

 寫作題目

With the advent of the Internet, how people go about their daily lives has been drastically changed.

As a matter of fact, people now live in a world where instant connection takes place all the time. People technically start the day with browsing the news on their mobile phones via the Internet, and finish with going to bed with their smart phones in hand.

With this change in habit, people are increasingly addicted to instant answers to anything and everything, since there is not a single thing that cannot be found through a simple internet search.

Do you think this instant connection that people are used to now is a good thing for humanity? Please share your thoughts.

1 教育

2 社會法律議題

3 民生生活

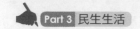
寫作技巧解析

　　題目說道，隨著網際網路的發展，人們日常生活的習慣也隨之劇烈地轉變，而事實上，現代人活在一個與網際網路沒有分界的世界，大部分的人一整天的開始與結束都與網路連結，但如此的連結，導致現代人習慣了快速的生活模式，這樣對人類的整體社會是好的嗎？以下範文採取正面支持立場，認為網路的快速，讓現代人能夠對不重要的瑣事「速戰速決」，以「get it over with」、「fast and furious」的效率，來提升生活品質。

應試撇步

　　範文提到，隨著科技發展，網際網路已「滲透 infiltrate」至生活中的各個層面，不論是「隨意地 at leisure」瀏覽網頁新聞，還是商業用途，人們已「習慣 be accustomed to」網際網路的「無遠弗屆 omnipresence」及快速連網的功能，而儘管有人質疑網路所帶來的「高步調 fast-paced」的生活，但範文採取支持立場，認為高速網路能幫助人們處理日常生活「瑣碎的 frivolous」的事物，能幫助人們的「時間管理 time management」。

 作文範例

🔊 MP3 034

1 教育

2 社會法律議題

3 民生生活

With today's technology, the Internet has infiltrated every aspect of our lives. Be it just browsing through the Internet at leisure for the latest news, or formally conducting one's business online, there is no denying that the Internet has become such an integral part of our daily lives that people are at risk of having a panic attack when deprived of access to the Internet. In addition to the omnipresence of the Internet, it is the speed that people have become so accustomed to that they would have a hard time adjusting otherwise. People revel in their ability to acquire instant connection to the online world. Despite the fact that some people reject to the fast-paced life style that the Internet has brought upon, I do stand in favor of such convenience brought by it, and will explain in the following paragraph.

隨著今日的科技發展，網際網路已經滲透至我們生活中的各個層面，不論是隨意、悠閒地瀏覽網路最新新聞，還是在網路上做生意，網際網路在我們生活中所扮演的核心角色是不置可否的，甚至許多人若被剝奪上網的權益時，將有可能引發恐慌症；而除了網路的無遠弗屆外，人們已非常習慣連線上網的速度，並樂於高速連網，要不然會難以適應，而儘管有些人反對網際網路所帶來的高步調生活，我個人卻是持贊成的立場、支持其所帶來的便利，且會在下一段詳加解釋。

For starters, being able to connect with the online world in a nanosecond exponentially increases people's efficiency at many tasks. One great example is the myriad of apps that have been invented to better facilitate this efficiency across a wide range of daily life functions. For instance, the apps introduced by the banking industry provide real-time information of a given bank account. This fast and furious way of either personal or business banking saves a lot of people's personal time to deal with frivolous financial matters. This greatly improves how people manage their time, and thus should be promoted.

首先，能夠秒連上網際網路的能力，大大地提升人們處理各個生活任務的效率，其中一個例子就是成千上萬已開發的手機應用程式，這些應用程式是用來驅動網路所帶來的效率，將其應用在生活各個領域，舉例來說，銀行業所開發的應用程式，這些程式能夠即時提供帳戶資訊，而這速戰速決的應用，不論是在個人還是企業帳戶上，都可節省處理瑣碎財務事項的時間，而這大幅地改善人們的時間管理，也因此更應當被開發。

In conclusion, life is generally composed of many frivolous but necessary tasks, and with the Internet, these tasks are easier than ever to get it over with. This, in turn, will make time management easier, and people more productive.

總結來說，人生通常有許多瑣碎、但卻無法避免的事情要處理，而因為有了網際網路，人們能夠對這些事物速戰速決，而也因為這樣，時間管理變得容易多了，且人們也可以更有生產力地來做其它事情。

1 教育

2 社會法律議題

3 民生生活

215

2 低頭族
by force of habit 積習成常

📖 成語閱讀故事

　　成語「積習成常」，其所形容的是對於某件事情，或某個行為，因為重複施做後，就成為自然而然的習慣了，其出處來自《水經註・溫水》中所言「暑褻薄日，自使人黑，積習成常，以黑為美。」，指出夏天使人膚色曬黑，而過了一段時間，大家習慣之後，也開始崇尚黝黑的膚色；在英文中，慣用語「by force of habit」即是用來形容某人做某件事情不用多加思索，有如反射動作般，因為這個行為已經做了很多次，也就是「積習成常」的意思。

With virtually everyone now owning a smartphone, there is a new term coined for those who constantly feel the need to check on their smart phones in various occasions.

Their eyes are always glued to smart phones when they are at family dinners, on transit through public transportation and so on.

The newly coined term "phubber" is a new word that is created through the combination of the world "phone" and the word "snubber," describing someone being nonchalant to their surroundings while much fixating on the content of their smart phones.

What do you think of this "phubber" social phenomenon? Please provide your rationale behind your view on this.

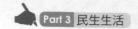

寫作技巧解析

　　題目說道，在現今人手一機的時代，出現了隨處可見的「低頭族」現象，而英文中，會用「phubber」這個新發明的單字來形容「低頭族」，而這個單字是由「phone」以及「snubber」這兩個單字組合而成，「snub」這個動詞是指「冷落別人」這個動作，而「snubber」即是「冷落別人的人」，合組後就是用來形容於各個場合用手機成癮的「低頭族」；以下範文採取反對「低頭族」成癮習慣的現象，並說明雖然「積習成常 by force of habit」，但應當嘗試打破此積習，鼓勵人們在外時應當更注意、珍惜身邊的人事物。

應試撇步

　　範文提到，在現今的年代，一般的「市井小民 average Joe or Jane」都是人手一機，也因為這樣，造成了低頭族現象「越來越普遍 ever more prevalent」，也讓人際關係間越加的「疏離 estranged」，並且「錯失 miss out on」生命中許多的美好事物，且就算在體驗各個社交活動的當下，其體驗也將「大打折扣 greatly diminished」，因為人們只顧「專注在 fixate on」手機上的內容及應用程式，而非眼前的人事物。

 作文範例

As we are now living in the kind of the world where an average Joe or Jane would always carry a personal smartphone to toy with for fun, the so-called "phubber" phenomenon is becoming ever more prevalent. A "phubber" refers to someone who shows a great deal of interest in their smartphone content so much that their eyes are practically glued to the screens at all times. The word "phubber" is a combination of the word "phone" and the word "snubber," taking the meaning out of the verb "snub" to portray the estranging behavior of individuals who are solely fixated on the virtual world rather than their physical surroundings.

我們正處在一個一般市井小民皆有手機為玩物的年代，而「低頭族」的現象也變得更為盛行，「低頭族」指的是某人過度沉溺於智慧型手機的內容及應用程式上，「低頭族」的英文為「phubber」，是「phone」跟「snubber」這兩個單字的綜合，取用「snub」這個動詞來詮釋個人因僅專注於手機的虛擬世界，而非他們自身所處的環境。

Granted, humans tend to do things by force of habit. This concept applies to both the ways people perceive and process information, and the physical behaviors of individuals. As for me, I do not view the behaviors of "phubbers" in a favorable light, mainly because I feel that they are missing out on things in life that could only be gained through physical experience. For these certain things in life, individuals need to actively engage in activities. Otherwise, what these activities are supposed to bring to individuals will be greatly diminished when participants are to be continuously interrupted by smartphone uses. For example, one's quality time with family members will not be as pleasurable if those who sit at the dinner table are constantly looking down to check messages on the phone.

理所當然，人類的行為舉止總是積習成常的，這個概念可通用在人們對於新知的認知，及內化吸收的過程，也可運用在人們具體的行為舉止上，而我並不贊同這些「低頭族」的行為，因為我認為他們的行為致使他們錯失生活中許多的美好事物，而這些事物只能透過親身體驗、積極地參與活動，才能有所得，要不然，當活動的參與者一直被智慧型手機上的各種程式打擾時，這些活動所理當帶來的體驗也將大打折扣，舉例來說，在某人與其家族成員的聚會上，若餐桌上的大家時常低頭查看各自手機上的最新訊息，這個聚會也將難以圓滿。

To conclude, I oppose the prevalence of today's "phubber" phenomenon. As they are always so focused on their phones, they would miss out on many good old things that people of the past are so carefully cherished at the time that phones had not been invented back then.

總結來說，我反對今日「低頭族」現象的擴散，因為當他們專注在自己的手機時，他們將錯過許多生命中的美好事物，而這些事物在以前手機尚未被發明的年代，可是被看重、好好珍惜的。

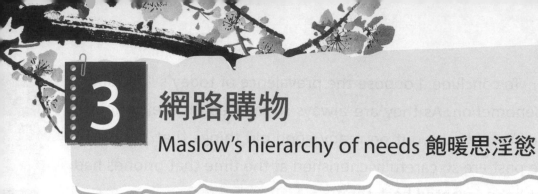

3 網路購物
Maslow's hierarchy of needs 飽暖思淫慾

📖 成語閱讀故事

　　成語「飽暖思淫慾」，字面上的意思，指的就是當人的最基本生理需求，如飲食、保暖等都能夠滿足時，就會有多餘的心思，來滿足更上一層的需求及慾望，儘管字面上是指有多餘的心思來滿足色慾，但其實可用來形容更廣的層面，如對於物質、奢侈品的慾望等；在英文中，可引用管理學中著名的「Maslow's hierarchy of needs」理論，來形容相同的概念，這理論基本上來說，認為人的需求分為五個等級，當較基本等級的需求能夠被滿足時，人們就會開始往上追求不同等級的需求，如歸屬感、關愛及物慾等。

寫作題目

In developed countries, the living standard has been lifted to a critical point where the majority of people do not need to worry about whether or not food is in sufficient supply, how to find a shelter on a rainy day and so on.

This, when coupled with the maturation of electronic commerce that is commonly referred to as E-commerce, would undoubtedly change people's lives in a radical manner.

As industry statistics indicate, online shopping is on the rise as people are finding and appreciating the convenience of buying things online only with mouse clicking while not needing to step outside the house.

What is your take on this trending phenomenon? Please explain.

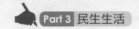

寫作技巧解析

　　題目說道，在已開發國家中，生活水平已提高，大部分的民眾不需擔心食物供給是否充沛，或是擔心下雨天時該去哪裡避雨，而這提高的生活水平，搭配網路購物的蓬勃發展，將劇烈地改變人們的生活；以下範文採取支持網路購物立場，並用成語「飽暖思淫慾」、管理學理論「Maslow's hierarchy of needs」來解釋，當民眾生活水平發展到一定境界，將會開始追求更高一層的需求滿足，而這也就是個自然的過程。

應試撇步

　　範文提到，開發中國家的人民，大部分有一定的生活水準，對於基本的民生需求，較能夠「自給自足 self-sufficient」，而統計顯示，「網路購物 online shopping」越加普及，民眾也越來越「習慣、適應 acclimatize」網路上虛擬商城的運作方式，並追求這「商業模式 business model」所提供的便利性，及找尋具有一定「品牌認知度 brand recognition」的優質商品，以造就其個人較高層面的需求滿足。

作文範例

🎵 MP3 036

In developed countries, the majority of people are living on a certain level of living standard. In other words, people in those nations are mostly self-sufficient enough to satisfy their basic human needs, such as to meet the minimum bodily requirement of nutrients intake and so on. As people in these societies have no need to worry about the fulfillment of such basic needs, it is natural progression that is in alignment of Maslow's hierarchy of needs for people to go after other pursuits that are ranked higher in Maslow's proposed structure of ranking for human needs.

在已開發國家中，其大部分人民的生活品質有一定的水準，換句話説，那些國家的人民通常在基本民生需求方面，皆可自給自足，比如説一般基本營養的補充、吸收，以符合身體的正常運作，而也因為這些社會中的人民不需為了是否能滿足其生活的基本需求而擔心，因此正如飽暖思淫慾所形容的，這些民眾開始追求其它較高階的人類需求，也只是正常的行為、現象而已。

One way to further facilitate the fulfillment of human needs on higher levels is through the booming development of the E-commerce. More specifically, people's acclimatization to the virtual realm of online shopping. As today's people are well-equipped to throw worries out of the window, worries on basic needs such as whether they are able to pay for the next meal, they are well prepared to pursue the fulfillment of higher needs, and in the case of online shopping, they are going after pursuits such as convenience, choosing quality products with desired brand recognition and so on. Since this is natural progression of human behaviors, I view the trending phenomenon of online shopping in a favorable light, and believe the booming business model could ultimately increase people's living standard even higher and more expansively across the globe, as E-commerce has the capability of providing cross-continent services to customers.

為滿足較高層次的需求，其中一個方法是利用電子商務的蓬勃發展，更確切地來說，也就是民眾對於網路購物消費模式的習慣，而當現代人民能夠不愁基本民生問題，比如說不需要擔心下一餐的著落，他們即可開始追尋更高層次需求的滿足，而以網路購物的例子來說，人民所追求的是方便、便利，及其喜愛品牌的優質商品等等，而既然這些需求的演化是自然的進展，我認同網路購物越加受歡迎的趨勢，且相信這蓬勃發展的商業模式，將更提升人民的生活水準，且能夠將進步帶到世界各地，因為電子商務是無遠弗屆的，能夠提供跨洲的服務。

In a nutshell, today's customer behavior of increased purchases online is a positive thing. As the society progresses forward, people's needs also change to reflect the level of development of the country they are in.

總結來説，現代消費者的網路購物行為是個正面的現象，因為隨著社會的進步，民眾的需求也應當隨之改變，以反映出他們所處國家的進步程度才是。

4 社交封閉

go big or go home 畫地自限

　　成語「畫地自限」，其字面上的意思是指某人在地面上劃清界線，而將自己限制在所畫的框線裡，因而出不來、不敢踰矩，其引申用來形容某人對於自己所能達到的成就設限，而因為這樣的心理因素，導致此人無法突破，沒有顯著的進步與成長；在英文中，常聽到「go big or go home」這句話，其所形容的即是對於每件事皆應全力以赴，因為若沒有卓越的表現的話，機會將逝去，最終也只能回到平凡的狀態、生活。換句話說，這句話也就是在鼓勵人們避免「畫地自限」，應當嘗試追求卓越。

寫作題目

With the development of technology, modern people enjoy the luxury of being able to complete virtually all daily tasks from the comfort of one's home, without the unavoidable requirement of one's physical presence necessary to carry out these tasks as before when technology had not been as advanced.

With this technological advancement, people of certain characteristics, take tech-savvy for example, are developing more distant relationships than before with family members, peers in social circles, work contacts and so on, as they can literally complete anything and everything without stepping out of their accommodations as long as there is an Internet connection.

What do you think of this social phenomenon? Please explain.

寫作技巧解析

　　題目說道，隨著科技的進步，現代人幾乎能夠在家裡即完成身邊的大小事，而不需像以前一樣必須出門才能夠處理事情，而也因為這樣的便利，有些人的社交圈也因此變得較為封閉；以下範文對此社會現象採取反對的立場，認為社交對於拓展人脈、促進生活豐富度等方面具有正面的影響，而面對人生的正確態度應為「go big or go home」，應當主動開拓社交圈，為自己創造機會，以避免「畫地自限」，而錯失實踐自我的可能。

應試撇步

　　範文提到，隨著科技進步發展所帶來的便利，致使現代某些人與他人之間，存在著「社交上離群索居 socially isolated」的現象，但「科學證實 scientifically proven」人的大腦先天「已被設計、設定 hard-wired」為需要藉由交際應酬、「面對面 face-to-face」的談話等活動來「刺激腦內思考、智力 cerebrally stimulate」、腦部，以利其分泌有助快樂指數的「腦內啡 endorphins」，並可藉由社交來認識新朋友、拓展人際，為自己的人生「開創更多機會 open doors」。

作文範例

MP3 037

With the advent of the Internet, people are becoming ever more independent of one another. In other words, they are perfectly capable of going about their daily business all on their own with only the help of an internet connection. For example, they can order groceries online, have them delivered to their doorsteps, pay all the bills on the Internet and so on. However, with this convenience also comes a trending phenomenon where a certain portion of the society is becoming socially isolated. One explanation behind such a phenomenon is that they do not have to be out and interact with people more frequently than they were in the past.

隨著網際網路的誕生，人們對於群體的相互依賴性已降低許多，換句話說，藉由網際連線的幫助，人們大半可靠自己來處理生活中的許多事物，比如說，人們可在網路上購買蔬果雜貨，並立即宅配到府，或是可於網路上付清帳單、欠款等等，然而，這樣的方便性也導致社會中某部分的個體越加與人群疏離，社交封閉的現象也更加顯著，而其中一個原因就是，比起以往人們已不需外出與人頻繁地互動，即可完成這些生活中的大小事。

My personal view on this trending phenomenon is not favorable. As people have been a social creature throughout the evolution of human history, it is scientifically proven that being social with other people is hard-wired in our brain anatomy. When we are not presented with opportunities to be socially engaged in face-to-face scenarios, our brains are not being cerebrally stimulated as they are inherently designed to respond positively to such social stimulations for an adequate amount of endorphins release. Produced by one's central nervous system, endorphins reportedly have the effect of strengthening one's resistance to pain as well as increasing one's level of happiness felt by individuals. Besides, meeting and maintaining strong relationships with people can open many doors to individuals in many ways, not just career-wise. Therefore, as the saying goes, "Go big or go home," we should all try to explore as many opportunities as possible in life, and meeting people is one of the greatest ways to achieve that goal.

我個人對此越加盛行的現象抱持著不支持的態度,因為人類自古演化以來,一直都是社交、群居的生物,而科學也證實,我們腦部的先天設計,決定人類生為社交動物的事實,所以,當我們沒有與人面對面交際的機會時,我們的腦部無法接受到適當的刺激及活化,而人類腦部的先天設計,就是鼓勵其多與他人接觸、交際,以刺激腦內啡的釋放,而腦內啡是由人類的中樞系統所釋出,在人類對於痛的阻抗力及快樂的程度上有著正面的影響;另外,多認識人

及保有健全的人際關係能為許多人開啟許多機會，且並不只是在工作方面有幫助而已，所以，切勿畫地自限，我們應當多方面嘗試各個機會，而與人見面是達成此目標的好方法之一。

In short, I do not think people should be limited to their house confinements despite advances in today's modern technology. As stated above, people should be as social as possible, both for the sake of their own happiness and for the potentially door-opening opportunities.

總結來説，儘管現今科技進步，我認為人們的活動範圍不應只局限在自己家裡，而如上所述，人類應當多參與社交活動，以利自己的快樂指數，以及為自己增加打開機會大門的機率。

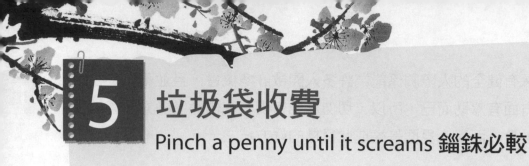

5 垃圾袋收費
Pinch a penny until it screams 錙銖必較

📖 成語閱讀故事

　　成語「錙銖必較」，形容某人對於金錢，或者對於一般事物、人際關係等各方面，計算得很仔細，也就是愛計較，連小細節也不放過，都要考慮、琢磨的意思，而在古時候，「錙」跟「銖」都是用來衡量重量的單位，但是這兩個衡量的計算單位皆很微小，也因此「錙銖必較」就被用來形容某人對於事物的態度小心、仔細，總是要斤斤計較的意思；在英文中，有句話「Pinch a penny until it screams.」，其字面上的意思為某人對於連「一分錢 penny」這價值相對較小的貨幣單位都十分看重、重視，甚至「緊抓著一分錢不放直到這一分錢開始尖叫」，用擬人化的説法來形容一分錢，也增添了一分趣味，而其也就是指某人「錙銖必較」的意思。

In Taiwan, the government is trying to regulate the level of how much of an amount that its population is collectively producing.

One way to do so is through the imposed fees that are specifically designed to curb wastes production. The fees are collected on the basis of how much of an amount one household normally produces.

There are a variety of ways to measure how much wastes each household generally produces on a periodic basis, and there are also quite a few controversies surrounding the fairness and accuracy of each measurement method.

How do you think of the government's policy and practice on collecting fees as an attempt to regulate wastes production? Please explain.

1 教育

2 社會法律議題

3 民生生活

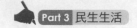
寫作技巧解析

　　題目提到，台灣政府嘗試透過垃圾袋隨袋徵收的政策來控制每戶的垃圾量，而對於所徵收的費用，儘管有許多各種不同的計算方法可以考慮採納、實施，但許多人對於這些計算方式帶有許多的質疑及爭議；以下範文採取正面支持的立場，認為對於垃圾袋收費的議題，政府的確應當「錙銖必較」，採取「Pinch a penny until it screams.」的立場，才能有效控制民眾所產出的垃圾量。

應試撇步

　　範文提到，為了響應「永續的 sustainable」及環保的風潮，政府決定來「管控 regulate」民眾的垃圾製造量，而其中一種較為被接受的作法，就是垃圾袋隨袋徵收的政策，此措施主張民眾購買垃圾袋的數量與他們實際製造的垃圾量有「相關連性 correlation」，所以，若掌握了民眾對於金錢的愛惜及考量，將能夠無形中降低個人，乃至社會整體的垃圾製造量。

 作文範例

🎧 MP3 038

In Taiwan, as the global trends towards preserving the environment and creating a more sustainable future for human offspring continue, the government is searching for effective ways to control its people's wastes production. One of these efforts to more effectively regulate the amount of people's garbage production is through enacted fees to collect money based on how much amount one household creates. As there are quite a few ways proposed to measure one's garbage production, one most commonly used method is to base the fees on how many garbage bags are purchased by individuals. This is a fair method as there should be a correlation between the amount of garbage production and the number of bags purchased for that creation.

在台灣，當全球趨勢注重在環境保存，以及為子孫後代創造永續未來的同時，政府正在找尋能夠有效控制人民垃圾製造量的方法，而其中一個可以有效掌控人民垃圾製造量的方法，是藉由所制定的垃圾量計量方式來收費，而儘管有許多能衡量個體垃圾製造量的提案，但最常被利用的方法為藉由個人所購買的垃圾袋數量來量計個人的垃圾製造量，因為垃圾袋的購買數量與實際垃圾製造量存在著相對應的因果關係，所以這個計量方式是被認為最公平、最具邏輯的。

I personally take a favorable view of this policy and practice. By charging additional fees on people's purchase of standard garbage bags of various sizes, the government takes advantage of people's general mindset to reduce unnecessary costs to increase savings. In other words, as the general public's mentality is mostly what is called "pinching a penny until it screams," the government successfully achieves its goal of reducing garbage amount produced by its countrymen. People will start being mindful of how they can decrease unneeded wastes production in order to consume lesser amount of garbage bags. Otherwise, they will need to spend more money on garbage bags if they do not curb the amount of their wastes production.

對於這樣的政策及措施，我個人抱持著支持的態度，因為當人民購買各尺寸的標準垃圾袋須多付費時，政府把握住了大部分人民的心態，那就是盡量減少不必要的開支、增加存款的心態，換句話說，當民眾整體抱持著「錙銖必較」的心態時，政府能夠藉由此措施來成功地減少其人民的垃圾製造量，因人們將開始注意其廢物製造量，以降低他們對於垃圾袋的需求，減少開銷。否則，他們如果不減少垃圾量，就得花更多錢在購買垃圾袋上。

All in all, I support the government's practice to collect extra fees on people's purchase of garbage bags. This practice will create a more sustainable future for generations to come, and ultimately make the world a better place to live in.

綜合來說，我贊同政府在人民購買垃圾袋的同時增加收費的措施，因為這樣能夠為後代創建永續的未來，並最終讓世界能夠享有更好的生活環境。

1 教育

2 社會法律議題

3 民生生活

239

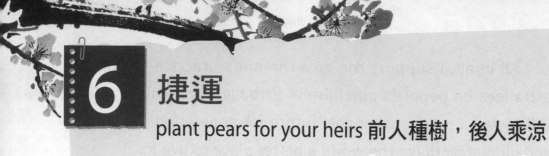

6 捷運
plant pears for your heirs 前人種樹，後人乘涼

成語閱讀故事

　　成語「前人種樹，後人乘涼」，簡單來說，其所形容的即是老一輩為後代努力建設、付出勞力的情事，為的就是讓後代子孫能夠享有更好的生活，促進未來社會的整體福祉；而在英文中，有句話「plant pears for your heirs」，其所形容的即是「前人種樹，後人乘涼」的意思，字面上的意思是指為「後代子孫 heirs」栽種、續種「梨子 pears」，其意象與「種樹」、「乘涼」相呼應，且「pears」與「heirs」兩個單字押韻，用在寫作文章內，不只可讓閱卷者瞭解考者生對英文及其慣用語的掌握，也增添了一分趣味。

寫作題目

Around all the global major cities, public transit system, be it New York City's subway or London's underground transit system, which is lovingly dubbed "the Tube" by locals and international visitors alike, is always an integral part of each city's urban development.

A well-designed and developed public transit system can bring about many long-lasting benefits for both the government's running of the city and its city dwellers' life quality.

However, the development process can be painstakingly long and can cause quite a few inconveniences for people during the system's construction period.

What is your take on this? Do you think it is worthwhile to invest the required time and resources on the system? Please explain.

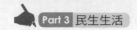

✚ 寫作技巧解析

　　題目提道，世界各國的大城市，不論是紐約市的地下鐵，還是倫敦外號為「管子」的地鐵系統，都將地鐵系統的開發及維護列為城市發展的重要目標、績效之一，而當然，設計良好的地鐵系統能夠為市府及市民帶來許多的利益，但建造的過程經常是非常冗長、且會暫時帶來許多的不便；以下範文採取支持地鐵系統建造的立場，並用「前人種樹，後人乘涼 plant pears for your heirs」來說明，若沒有今天的付出，社會將無法進步，因此應當將眼光放遠，為未來的福祉設想。

◎ 應試撇步

　　範文提到，世界各國的主要城市，皆將「大眾運輸系統 public transit system」列為城市發展的重要目標，因為此系統不只能夠「提升 elevate」人民的生活品質，也可在環保方面降低汙染及路上「交通阻塞 traffic congestion」的現象，而雖然大眾運輸系統可帶來諸多好處，有些人仍「質疑 be skeptical of」其建設的必要性，認為時間及資源的花費過大，但是範文說道，「一分耕耘，一分收穫 no pains, no gains」，此時擴建的辛勞，將可造福後代，創造更多的社會福祉。

 作文範例

1 教育

2 社會法律議題

3 民生生活

Around the globe, all the major cities have some sort of public transport system, take Taipei city's MRT for example. This kind of development is always a focal point for each major city's urban planning worldwide. Granted, the public transport system could elevate the level of convenience both for local city dwellers and travelers visiting from abroad. In addition, the system is also instrumental in the government's efforts to make advancements on the environmental front, as a good public transit system with affordable fares can very much effectively lower the everyday use of personal means of transportation, which is usually cars, and can in turn decrease air pollutions and traffic congestions.

　　世界各地的大城市皆有各自的大眾運輸系統，比如說台北的捷運系統就是其中一個例子，而這些大眾運輸系統是各個城市每年度城市發展規劃裡的重要項目之一，而理所當然，這些大眾運輸系統能夠提升當地市民及國外旅客的生活、旅遊的便利，並且，能夠幫助政府增進環保，因為好的大眾運輸系統，搭配合理的價格，能夠有效地降低每日私人車的用量，而間接地降低汙染及交通阻塞的問題。

However, as much as many benefits that a public transit system is capable of bringing, the planning and construction process can take an incredible amount of time and consume many available resources from the government. As a result, some are skeptical of the necessity of building and expanding such a transit system. I personally support the time and efforts that a government is committing to constructing the system, despite the temporary inconvenience and the large amount of invested resources. This kind of upfront investment is necessary as the saying goes, "no pains, no gains." The investment can essentially be viewed as planting pears for your heirs.

然而，儘管大眾運輸系統能夠帶來許多的便利，其計畫及建造的過程通常會花上許多的時間及政府的可用資源，也因為這樣，有些人會質疑建造、擴建此系統的需要性，我個人則是支持政府將時間及資源用在此系統的建造上，儘管會對現在的居民造成一時的不便，並會花上許多資源，但就像諺語說的：「一分耕耘，一分收穫」，這也是人生中不變的道理，所以人們應當嘗試著以長遠的計畫來思考，以前人種樹，後人乘涼之姿，為後代考量利益。

In conclusion, people should be able to sacrifice their temporary convenience for the improvements that would be brought to the living quality of coming generations though constructing a transit system. After all, it is people's interest, collectively speaking, to move forward with advancements on all fronts rather than being stagnant with the status quo.

總結來說，人們應當要能夠犧牲自己一時的生活便利性，以換取大眾運輸系統所能帶給後代生活品質方面的進步，畢竟，整體來說，人們應當期許社會能夠持續往前進，在各方面進步、突破，而不應只在原地打轉、自滿才是。

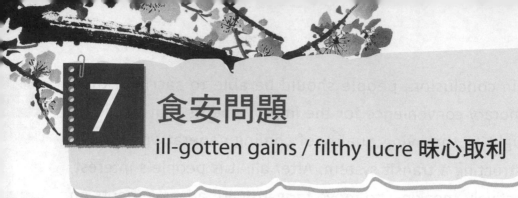

7 食安問題
ill-gotten gains / filthy lucre 昧心取利

　　成語「昧心取利」，其所形容的是指商人或企業，明知道其所提供的服務或是產品有瑕疵，還是為了賺取金錢及利益，而不顧道德的規範，將這些服務及商品提供、販賣給民眾；在英文中，會用「ill-gotten gains」或是「filthy lucre」來形容不肖商人透過不法、或是不道德的途徑所賺取的金錢利益，「ill-gotten」即是指「透過不法途徑而得」，而「filthy lucre」中的「lucre」即是指「金錢」，搭配「filthy 骯髒的」，暗指不肖商人透過不道德、「昧心取利」的方式來賺取的錢財。

1 教育

2 社會法律議題

3 民生生活

In the history of commercial world, there is no shortage of stories about businesses that are conducted in a dishonest way. They do so mainly as a means to trade for substantial profits.

Still around the globe, there are thousands of cases depicting what is essentially the same story of dishonest behaviors in business, take the collapse of Lehman Brothers for example.

With that said, the issue of food safety in Taiwan had just been coming into light. People are made aware of the potential hazardous additives to health found in many a food product.

What is your view on this? Please explain.

寫作技巧解析

　　題目說道，在商業的世界中，有數以萬計的案例記載著各行各業中不法獲利、不道德的行為，比如說雷曼兄弟的倒閉等，而在台灣，食安問題一直到這幾年才開始「見光 come into light」；以下範文對於不肖商人為了獲取暴利，而「昧心取利」，將民眾的安全、健康顧慮擺一邊，以獲取「ill-gotten gains」、「filthy lucre」的行為感到不恥，並建議政府應當嚴加把關，以捍衛民眾的食安權益。

應試撇步

　　範文提到，許多企業從事「不道德的 unethical」的行為，以「換取 in exchange of」較高的利潤，而台灣的食品業也不例外，某些黑心企業選取低成本、品質有疑慮的食材，以賺取利差的行為，是令人感到「可恥的 despicable」，而儘管大眾有意願「抵制 boycott」這些黑心食品，但真正有效的措施，應當是由政府主動來制訂相關的法律，將黑心企業「繩之以法、使其負法律責任 legally hold someone accountable」，以杜絕日後再犯的機率。

 作文範例

MP3 040

In many parts of the world, news that report on dishonest businessmen engaging in unethical business activities in exchange of great fortune can be constantly found. In Taiwan, the food industry is no exception, as numerous scandalous reports that shed light on the food safety issue made headlines in the past couple of years. The persistent reoccurrence of news reports on hazardous additives that are found in numerous food products is a serious matter. From this, the conduct of choosing ingredients at a lower cost, but of a potentially detrimental nature to human health, is unethical and should be corrected sooner rather than later.

在世界各地，有關不肖商人為了賺取暴利，而從事不法、不道德的商業行為的新聞時有所聞，而在台灣，食品產業也是其中一個案例，而這可從過去幾年內，許多關於食品安全議題的頭版新聞看出端倪，而有關食品添加物危害健康的報導未曾間斷，這本身即是個嚴重的議題，而其中，商人選擇較低成本，但有危害人體健康疑慮的食材原料，是不道德的行為，而此行為應當被及早糾正、改正才是。

Personally, I find the behavior despicable because certain businessmen in the food industry can so willingly disregard people's health conditions only to achieve greater margins of profit on their companies' products. The profits earned this way are indeed ill-gotten gains, which should be looked down upon by the whole society. However, there is not much the general public can do to try to boycott against these unethical companies' products. Rather, the real power lies in the government's hand to pass stringent laws to avoid businesses earning filthy lucre through legal loopholes again, and to protect people's rights to safe, health-beneficial food products.

　　我個人的觀點認為，某些食品產業的不肖商人願意犧牲民眾的健康，以換取較大的利潤，是很可恥的行為，而商人這種昧心取利，以獲得不法利潤的行為，應當被社會唾棄、鄙視。然而，社會大眾對於這些黑心企業所採取的抵制行為，影響力也是有限，因此，政府應當介入，制訂較嚴謹的法律條文，以防企業再度鑽法律漏洞、昧心取利，確保民眾權益，使其能夠享有安全，且對健康有益的食品。

In conclusion, I think the government should step in to legally hold those who conduct unethical businesses accountable. Otherwise, this kind of behavior will not be effectively stopped, and more businessmen would also engage in the pursuit of filthy lucre in the future.

總結來說，我認為政府應當適時介入，以將這些黑心企業繩之以法。要不然，這些黑心的行為無法有效地被制止，未來也將有更多商人仿效、昧心取利地追求財富。

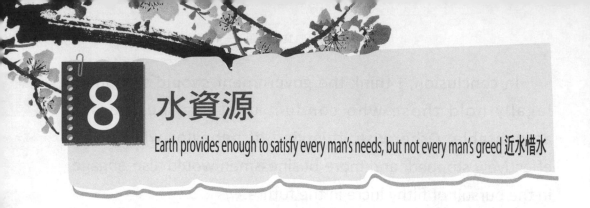

8 水資源

Earth provides enough to satisfy every man's needs, but not every man's greed 近水惜水

成語閱讀故事

　　成語「近水惜水」，其字面上的意思是指，儘管某人所處之地靠近水源，但仍然很珍惜、愛惜身邊唾手可得的資源，也就是用來形容某人有愛護資源及節儉的美德；在英文中，印度國父甘地曾説過一句經典名言：「Earth provides enough to satisfy every man's needs, but not every man's greed.」，其背後的寓意，即與「近水惜水」相似，説明儘管地球足以提供每個人存活所需的資源，但卻無法滿足每個人對於資源使用上的貪婪，其所傳達的，就是若人類都能滿足、珍惜現有資源，而不會因為欲望，或自己一時的便利，而浪費資源的理想。

寫作題目

As with any natural resources on the planet, there are certain risks that can occur when these resources are not appropriately managed for human consumption.

The main challenge lies in the fact that the amount of these resources is oftentimes limited. As a result, if not managed with carefulness, these resources are at the risk of depletion or being permanently and irreversibly damaged.

Among these issues, the issue of water resources is arguably the most important one as water is an inseparable part of our daily lives. However, as drinking water is available to those who live in developed countries, it is indeed a scarce resource for those who love in developing countries, take certain parts in the continent of Africa for example.

What is your view on this? Please explain.

1 教育

2 社會法律議題

3 民生生活

寫作技巧解析

　　題目說道，人類在利用地球上的許多資源時，應妥善規劃，要不然大部分的資源皆不是能夠予取予求的，若在使用上沒有事先計畫，很有可能將面臨資源耗竭、走到無法復原的局面；以下範文採正面立場，鼓吹應善用現代科技，為開發中國家也能帶來足夠的乾淨水資源，供其人民飲用，並藉由成語「近水惜水 Earth provides enough to satisfy every man's needs, but not every man's greed.」這句話來警惕已開發國家的人民，應好好珍惜、愛惜身邊充沛的飲用水資源，以避免過度浪費。

應試撇步

　　範文提到，在現今這個年代，仍有許多人無法獲取足夠的「飲用水 drinkable water、drinking water」，而在沒有乾淨的飲用水資源的環境下，人們若「啜飲、大口喝下 gulp」這些不乾淨的水，其「感染、患染 contract」上「痢疾 dysentery」的風險將大增，並且將出現「腹瀉 diarrhea」等症狀，而還好現代科學家發明了許多「裝置 apparatus」來幫助非洲民眾享有更多可飲用的水資源，且最後文末也提醒身在已開發國家中的我們，應當近水惜水，好好珍惜身邊的水資源。

 作文範例　　　　　　　　　　　🔘 MP3 041

Even in today's world, those who live in developing countries are still having limited, scarce access to clean drinkable water. This poses a serious problem as people require a certain level of water consumption to sustain their daily functioning. What's more, unclean resources of water can easily take away people's lives as they take gulps of water from unsafe sources in parts of certain developing countries. In Africa, people can often contract, and consequently die of, dysentery from drinking unclean water. Those who have contracted dysentery display symptoms of diarrhea, which can further pollute the conditions of water sources in these countries and essentially create a vicious cycle.

即便在現代，某些生活在開發中國家的人民，身邊的可飲用水資源還是不夠充足，而這是一個很嚴重的問題，因為人們需要一定程度的攝水量，才能維持正常的生理運作，況且，在某些開發中國家內，若人們飲用不乾淨的飲用水時，不只會危害自己的健康，甚至可因此失去性命。就如在非洲，人們容易因飲用了不乾淨的飲用水而感染痢疾，並因此喪生，而這些感染痢疾的人，會經常有腹瀉的症狀，這些症狀將更加汙染其所在地的水資源，形成了惡性的循環。

To solve this water crisis in Africa, I personally support many charitable organizations' efforts to bring clean, safe drinkable water to every corner of the continent. Among these efforts, there are a few breakthroughs made by modern scientists to bring easy-to-use, low-cost apparatuses to those who otherwise do not have easy access to clean drinking water. One of these tools is the product named "LifeStraw," which has the capability to filter and purify water from unclean sources to clean, drinkable state. This way, water with pollutants and harmful bacteria can be easily cleansed through "LifeStraw," and thus available for drinking in a matter of seconds.

我個人支持許多的公益團體，為了解決非洲大陸水資源危機而做的努力，而在這些的努力、嘗試中，現代科學家也帶來了許多的突破，他們發明了許多簡易好用、低成本的裝置，來幫助人民方便地享用可飲用水資源，而其中一項裝置是名為「生命飲管」的產品，它能夠過濾、淨化不乾淨的水源至乾淨、可飲用的狀態，這麼一來，充滿汙染物及細菌的水源將能夠藉由「生命飲管」，在幾秒鐘內簡易地淨化為可飲用的水源。

With the above said, those who are lucky enough to live in developed countries should cherish drinkable water resources that are readily available in their lives. As Gandhi once said, "Earth provides enough to satisfy every man's needs, but not every man's greed." Those in developed countries should cherish those resources at their fingertips even more, as there are indeed others struggling for the same thing right on the other side of the world.

綜合上述，已開發國家的人民，應當珍惜其生活中唾手可得的飲用水資源，並且體現「近水惜水」的精神。如甘地所說的：「地球足以提供每個人存活所需的資源，但卻無法滿足每個人對於資源使用上的貪婪。」那些已開發國家的人民，應當好好愛惜手邊的資源，因為在地球的另一端，可能有人正為了同樣的資源而煩惱、掙扎。

9 空氣汙染
daylight robbery 豐取刻與

📖 成語閱讀故事

　　成語「豐取刻與」，其出處來自《荀子‧君道》中所提及的「上好貪利，則臣下百吏乘是而後豐取刻與，以無度取千民。」其字面上的意思是指君王從人民身上收取的多，如稅賦、勞力等資源，但人民所獲取的回饋，卻不符合比例原則，也就是剝削的意思；在英文中，當某人認為在某交易情況下，他們所被收取的價碼或條件是極不合理的，會用「daylight robbery」這個慣用語來形容此交易，而籌碼交換的不公平，使購買人感到被剝削、「豐取刻與」的感覺。

 寫作題目

Around the world, people are paying more attention to the ways that can make the world a greener place to live in.

Among the many environmental problems that our world faces today, air pollution is a serious one. There are many forms of air pollution, and one of the most noticeable would be the existence of smog.

This kind of pollution can not only wreak havoc on our planet, but also bring serious damage to our health. Therefore, the Taiwanese government is making efforts to reduce the level of air pollution.

What is your view on this? Please explain.

1 教育

2 社會法律議題

3 民生生活

寫作技巧解析

　　題目說道，在世界各地，越來越多人開始注重如何能夠讓地球成為一個適合人類居住的綠世界，而在現今的世界中，空氣汙染可說是眾多汙染問題中很嚴重的一個議題，因為空氣污染不只破壞環境，更會影響人類的身體健康；以下範文採取支持立場，認為儘管台灣政府在許多建設方面對人民可說是「豐取刻與」，但在改善空汙這一塊，可由現今台北市街頭隨處可見的綠化空間可知，人民繳納的稅在這方面如「daylight robbery」般，看不到政府努力的結果。

應試撇步

　　範文提到，空氣汙染是個嚴重的議題，而空汙有許多形式，有容易觀察到的「霾害 smog」，也有較「不易察覺，但有潛在危害 insidious」的形式的空汙，如某些「懸浮粒子 particles」若「累積、組成 amass」至一定程度後，將會對環境產生永久的傷害，而台灣政府對於空汙的處理有效，並以台北為例，將許多廢棄區域「活化 rejuvenate」，改建為公開的公共綠空間供民眾使用，也促進「光合作用 photosynthesis」的運行。

 作文範例

Around the globe, air pollution is a serious problem that needs to be dealt with caution and seriousness. There are many forms of air pollutions, and some are more visible, while others are more of an insidious nature. For example, smog is one of the visible forms of air pollution. On the other hand, certain particles or substances, such as carbon dioxide are the kind of air pollution that no significant difference would be easily detected at the early stages, but when such substances amass over a certain level of amount, damages on the environment can be lasting and irreversible.

在世界各地，空氣汙染是個很嚴重的問題，應當謹慎、認真以待。空氣汙染有許多不同的形式，而有些是較顯而易見的，有些則是較難以察覺，但帶有潛在危害的。舉例來說，霾害就是較顯而易見的空汙例子，而另一方面，某些特定的懸浮微粒，比如說二氧化碳，就是空汙中一開始不易察覺，但當累積到一定程度後，將會對環境造成永久、不可逆危害的例子。

With air pollution being such a serious issue, the Taiwanese government is tackling the issue of air pollution head on. I support the government's conscious efforts to make some of the country's urban areas greener with clean air, take the capital city of Taipei for example. In Taipei, the level of air pollution has been effectively reduced in comparison to the quality of air decades ago. There are much more plants and trees being planted along the streets to purposefully integrate more greenery into the city's urban development. There are countless examples of deserted areas being rejuvenated and transformed into open public green space that not only provides a safe place for people to hang out, but also enables the interaction of the photosynthesis to counter with harmful elements resulting from air pollution.

當空汙是如此嚴重的議題時，台灣的政府也不遺餘力，直接面對這個問題。而我也支持台灣政府，其嘗試將這個國家的都市區域，朝向綠化的方向發展的努力，就拿台北市來説，台北的空氣污染程度，跟十年前相比，已大幅度地降低，而現今的路旁也規劃種植了許多的植物及樹木，目的就是將綠化的空間能夠成功融入城市的規劃及發展，並且，有許多廢棄區域被活化，轉化為公開的大眾綠色空間，不只提供了民眾休閒的安全去處，也使得光合作用的運行足以抵抗導因於空氣污染而產生的有害元素。

In conclusion, I support the government's efforts to mitigate the level of air pollution. On this front, people would, for once, be gladly paying their taxes and would not consider these sometimes exorbitant amounts of taxes to be daylight robbery by their government, as long as the government keeps up the good work they have been doing in tackling the problem of air pollution.

總結來説，我支持政府處理空氣汙染的努力，而在這個議題上，人們也難得對於繳税沒有怨言，沒有感到如被豐取刻與的無奈，而只要求政府能夠繼續保持在空汙這方面的進步、努力即可。

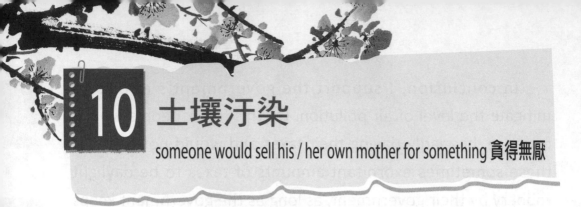

10 土壤汙染

someone would sell his / her own mother for something 貪得無厭

成語閱讀故事

　　成語「貪得無厭」是用來形容某人的欲望沒有限制，個性貪婪，其出處來自《左傳・昭公二十八年》中所提及的「貪婪無厭，忿類無期。」在英文中，有許多不同的慣用語來表達「貪得無厭」的意思，比如説，可以用「someone would sell his / her own mother for something」這句話來表示某人極渴望某個東西，到了願意不擇手段奪取、獲取那樣東西的地步，以滿足他們各自貪婪的欲望。另外，也常聽到「Pigs get fat, hogs get slaughtered.」這句諺語，警示人們不要「貪得無厭」，以免因為過度貪心，而造就了自己的失敗。

 寫作題目

Around the world, the issue of soil contamination is gaining lots of attention from the environmentalists and the government officials.

There are a variety of causes that can potentially worsen the land's pristine conditions, but the majority of them are man-made, as withering plants or animal carcasses in the wild would only benefit and fertilize the soil.

There are many serious ramifications that can be traced back to soil pollution as the main root cause. For example, people's health may be at risk after consuming supplies of food that are harvested out of contaminated soil.

Please share your own thoughts on the impact of soil pollution.

⊕ 寫作技巧解析

　　題目說道，在世界各地，土壤汙染的問題越來越受到關注，而土壤汙染本身有許多不同的成因，但主要都是由人類活動所造成的，因為枯萎的植物及動物的「屍體 carcass」並不會傷害土地，反倒是使土壤更加肥沃。以下範文支持政府推廣環保的努力，並呼籲大眾不要重蹈前人的覆轍，如在工業革命時，人類為了滿足其「貪得無厭」的私欲，而不停地開發、擴張，當時「Greedy factory owners would sell their own mothers for substantial profits and more expansion.」，就算過程中污染了土地也不介意，但最終將如「Pigs get fat, hogs get slaughtered.」所說，影響到的將會是人類自己的存活。

⑤ 應試撇步

　　範文提到，「土壤汙染 land contamination、land pollution」的主要成因為「人為的 man-made」，而在工業革命的時代，人們當時沒有現今的環保概念，因此總是貪婪、盡情地「掠奪 raid on」地球的資源，也因此對環境中原本「潔淨的 pristine」的土壤造成了很大的傷害。所以，現代人應當從日常生活中開始，實踐對土壤汙染有益的舉動，如不用塑膠袋、不喝「瓶裝水 bottled water」等等，以維護環境。

作文範例　　　　　　　　　　　　　　🔘 MP3 043

Around the globe, incidents of land contamination are constantly reported in the news. Sadly, many of the pollution sources for land contamination are man-made, as opposed to natural causes. To put it simply, in the process of people searching for ways to better their lives, the advancement of human society is often realized at the expense of the pristine land. However, as environmentalists are now drawing more attention to the issue, governments around the world are enacting policies and educating their citizens on how they can avoid polluting the land when going about their daily lives. Below are some examples of how people can help reduce the level of land pollution without compromising the advancement of human society.

在世界各地，土壤汙染的事件時有所聞，然而，不幸的是，許多土壤污染的來源都是人為的因素，而非自然的因素。簡單來説，在人類努力增進自己生活福祉的過程中，人類社會的進步，其實許多時候，是藉由犧牲了純淨的土地而換來的，不過，所幸在今日環保份子的努力下，各國政府也越加關注有關政策的制訂，及如何能夠教導民眾在生活中降低對於土壤的汙染，而接下來是一些能夠降低土壤汙染的範例，並且在同一時間，也不會妥協人類增進社會福祉的機會。

Firstly, in the period of the Industrial Revolution, people were not so educated on the potential effect of them exploiting the planet for resources. At the time, people were mostly looking out for themselves, aggressively going after ways to expand their wealth. Back then, greedy factory owners would sell their own mothers for substantial profits and more expansion. Nevertheless, ignorance is no longer an excuse for humankind, as we have come to realize the fact that there will be consequences if we just recklessly grab resources as we please. Some examples that we can help decrease soil contamination are to reduce unnecessary wastes in our daily lives, not to use plastic bags, not to purchase bottled water but just simply purify tap water for drinking, and so on.

首先，我們須瞭解，人類在工業革命時期的當下，並不瞭解掠奪地球資源的潛藏後果，所以在當下，大部分人都以自己的利益為重，積極地擴展財富，而當時許多的工廠主人，時常為了更多的利潤及擴張，而不擇手段、貪得無厭。當然，人類現在已無法再以無知為後盾，因為我們已知若我們繼續以莽撞的行為，並且以自我為中心的心態來掠奪資源的話，是要付出代價的。要幫助降低土壤汙染的話，我們可從降低生活中不必要的浪費、不使用塑膠袋、避免買瓶裝礦泉水，純喝淨化的自來水等行為開始著手，都可有效幫助降低土壤的汙染。

In conclusion, I support the efforts made by the governments to educate people on how to decrease the level of soil pollution. As the saying goes, "pigs get fat, hogs get slaughtered." If human beings keep raids on the planet's resources to simply satisfy their insatiable greed, they will only bring destruction unto themselves in the end.

　　總結來說，我支持政府教育民眾應如何降低土壤汙染的努力。因為就像諺語說的「人心不足蛇吞象，偷雞不著蝕把米」，要是人類繼續以貪得無厭的方式，掠奪地球資源的話，最終將只會帶來人類自己的毀滅。

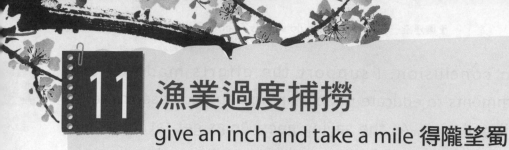

11 漁業過度捕撈
give an inch and take a mile 得隴望蜀

成語閱讀故事

　　成語「得隴望蜀」，其中的「隴」所指的是大陸甘肅那一帶，而「蜀」則是指四川那一帶的地區，其出處來自《後漢書‧岑彭傳》中所提到的「人苦不知足，既平隴，複望蜀，每一發兵，頭鬢為白。」所形容的即是某人貪得無厭，得到、滿足了某個欲望後，就會開始追求、想要更多，沒有極限；在英文中，時常會聽到「give an inch and take a mile」，雖然這句話通常是用來形容某人得寸進尺的行為，但其形容某人得到一「吋 inch」後，若沒有被制止，就會追求另一個境界，從一「吋」提升到一「里」，實猶如「得隴望蜀」般，欲望無止盡。

In some parts of the world, the issue of overfishing has been so out of hand that international organizations has to step in to bring awareness to those fishing practices.

In fact, there are many serious problems associated with overfishing practices, take the unbalanced ecosystem resulting from the overkilling of sea fish for example.

In other words, when people use fishing methods that would aggressively catch all the fish available in the area, there is a potential that certain stocks of fish species would soon drop below levels that would pose a threat to existing, balanced ecosystem.

What is your view on this? Please explain.

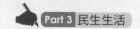

寫作技巧解析

　　題目問道，在某些地區，漁業過度捕撈的現象頻傳，有時甚至嚴重到國際組織須出手協助、協調的地步，而漁業的過度捕撈，對於人類社會來說，會帶來許多衝擊，比如說會造成生態系統失衡等等；以下範文採取反面立場，反對漁業過度捕撈的現象，並說明應嚴懲過度捕撈的業者，以免「give an inch and take a mile」的現象產生，並杜絕這些業者以不法途徑來滿足其「得隴望蜀」心態的企圖，進而維護生態及環境的平衡。

應試撇步

　　範文提到，「漁業過度捕撈 overfishing」對於地球的「生物多樣性 biodiversity」會「造成威脅 pose a threat to something」，而過度捕撈背後的動機，通常都是被「金錢、財富的回饋 monetary rewards」所驅使，並且以鯊魚被割鰭、丟回海裡的例子，說明有些人能夠為了金錢，而以殘忍及「不人道 inhumane」的方式來掠奪海底資源。最後說道，若要有效制止這種行為，相關法規須更嚴謹，才不會讓貪婪的人有機會「得隴望蜀」，進而得寸進尺。

 作文範例

🎵 MP3 044

In certain parts of the world, practices of overfishing have posed a serious threat to the completeness of the Earth's biodiversity. The reduced completeness of biodiversity can bring irreversible damages to the existing ecosystem, and therefore should be treated seriously. In my personal opinion, I am appalled by the lengths people are willing to go to in these fishing expeditions. Those who overfish are mostly doing so only for monetary rewards. They are so driven by money that they are willing to overfish in cruel and inhumane ways, only for their own benefit of profits expansion.

在世界某些地區，漁業過度捕撈的現象將會對地球的生物多樣性造成威脅，生物多樣性完整度的缺陷會為生態系統帶來不可逆的損壞，因此這個問題需要認真被看待。而我個人的觀點認為，某些人為了獲取錢財而不擇手段的手法是很可怕的，那些人多半是為了財富而過度捕撈魚類。他們為了自己錢財的擴張，而願以殘忍、不人道的手法來捕魚，這個現象是很讓人驚駭的。

One of these cruel and inhumane practices employed by some in the fishing industry includes the treatment of sharks. In certain regions, sharks are caught and their fins are cut off on the spot. What's worse, as the fins are the most valuable part on the body of sharks, many of those sharks are tossed right back into the deep sea. This is probably one of the purest forms of exploitation on these creatures as the sharks are essentially left to die when stripped of fins in the sea, unable to swim. To effectively bring this kind of exploitation to an end, governments and international organizations should work together to prevent overfishing from happening ever again.

這些殘酷、不人道的漁業捕撈現象，其中一個例子就是對於鯊魚的迫害。在某些地區，人們捕抓鯊魚，並當場將鰭割下，因為這些鰭是鯊魚身上最獲利的部位，但更糟的是，這些鯊魚之後就被丟回深海裡，這實在可說是人類對於其他生物剝削手段的極致案例之一了，因為這些失去鰭的鯊魚，也失去了牠們在其原本棲息的深海裡生存的能力，所以本質上來說，牠們根本就是被棄置在深海裡自生自滅、等待死亡；若要有效地杜絕這類對海底生物的剝削手段，政府及國際組織應當同心協力，一同防止漁業過度捕撈的現象再度發生。

In short, governments and international organizations should take a tougher stance on the issue of overfishing. Otherwise, the current regulations are somewhat too lax for those who are eager to exploit for profits. In the end, if not treated with more stringent laws, it will just be another typical situation where people are given an inch, and they take a mile.

簡短來説，政府及國際組織應當以更嚴厲的態度來看待漁業過度捕撈的議題。要不然，若不將相關規定制訂得更嚴謹的話，現今相對較鬆散的法規，將會使貪婪的人有機會得隴望蜀，持續他們過度捕撈的行為，以賺取更多的財富。

1 教育

2 社會法律議題

3 民生生活

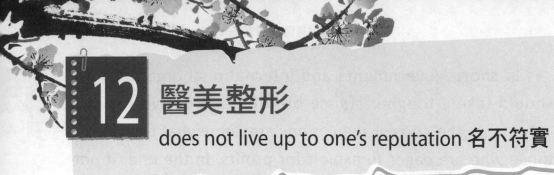

12 醫美整形

does not live up to one's reputation 名不符實

成語閱讀故事

　　成語「名不符實」，其所形容的是某人的名聲及形象與其本質不符，帶有暗指某人虛假、　君子的意味；在英文中，時常聽到某人或某事「does not live up to one's reputation」，其意思就是指某人、某事「名不符實」，與傳聞中的「名聲 reputation」並「不相符 does not live up to」另外，也常聽到「All that glitters is not gold.」這句話，字面上的意思是指，並不是每個「閃閃發亮glitter」的東西，都是貨真價實的黃金，很多時候，外在的表象與真實的內在，皆是不相符的，而其背後的意涵就是在說明現實中常見「名不符實」的現象、狀況。

Around the world, the practices of cosmetic surgery are being ever more accepted by the masses.

In some societies, it is even considered a great virtue when someone chooses to go under the knife only to make themselves more pleasing to the eye, take South Korea for example.

In fact, there are many types of cosmetic surgeries that are tailored to different parts of the body in today's world, and with the advancement of technology, people are offered a myriad of non-intrusive, painless options to easily tweak appearances to their own likings.

What is your view on the prevalence of cosmetic surgeries? Please explain.

⊕ 寫作技巧解析

　　題目問道，在世界各地，社會大眾越來越接受醫美整型的風潮，甚至像在南韓等國家，認為接受醫美整型的手術，能讓自己的外型加分，是值得鼓勵的，而隨著科技的進步，民眾現今擁有了更多非侵入性、無痛等手術選項，更加強化了醫美的風潮。以下範文採支持立場，認為只要是以安全為前提，且能增加個人自信，醫美整型是值得鼓勵的，然而，文章中也提到，儘管一般社會大眾著重在一個人的外在，但內在也應隨著外在美提昇，以免發生「名不符實 does not live up to、All that glitters is not gold.」的事情發生。

◎ 應試撇步

　　範文提到，人們願意「以各種形式 in any shape or form」來改善自己的外在美，其背後有各個不同的原因，而「根據自己的喜好 to one's own liking」來「動手術 go under the knife」改善外表，並不是一件不好的事，但「前提是 on the premise of」須以安全至上為原則，而文章也以美國施打「肉毒桿菌 Botox」為例，說明現在不只中熟年齡層風行肉毒桿菌的「施打 injection」，甚至年輕人也熱愛，因為據說定期地施打將會有「防止 preventative」老化的效果。

 作文範例

Around the world, people are getting more and more conscious of how they look. As a result, the number of people turning to plastic surgeons for ways to improve their appearances, literally in any shape or form, is increasing. There are a variety of reasons why people are willing to go under the knife to enhance their beauty. Whatever the reason, I feel it is perfectly acceptable for people to alter their appearance to their own likings, but only on the premise of ensured safety.

在世界各地，人們越加重視自己的外表，而也因為這樣，循求醫美整型，以各種形式為自己外在加分的人，其比率也越來越高，而人們之所以願意動刀、接受手術以改善外在容貌，背後有許多不同原因。不論原因為何，我認為接受手術以改變自己外型的行為，是完全可以接受的，但前提是要先確保安全才行。

With today's surgical improvement, people have access to a much safer choice of surgical procedures. Nowadays, some surgical techniques even make the idea of painless operations possible. This reduced pain, coupled with the improved, shortened recovery time, boosts people's interests in resorting to cosmetic surgeries for their preferred looks. For example, it is very popular for people, even those at a relatively younger ages such as their mid-thirties, to go for Botox injections in the United States. For those young people who go for shots of Botox on a regular basis, they believe such injections will yield some sort of preventative effects. Essentially, they believe that receiving regular shots of Botox at a younger age can ultimately slow the pace of aging on their looks.

今日手術科技的進步，讓人們能夠享有更安全的醫美整型手術，甚至有無痛手術的選項，而其降低的手術疼痛感，以及更快速的術後復元期間，讓人們對於醫美的需求量大增。舉例來說，在美國有許多人，包括年紀在三十區間的輕熟年齡層，都很風行藉由肉毒桿菌來維持外貌，並且認為年輕時定期地施打肉毒桿菌，能夠有效延緩外表的老化。

In general, I support people's efforts to increase their level of confidence through plastic surgeries, but only on the premise of ensured safety. On the other hand, as the saying goes, "All that glitters is not gold." People need to also work on their inner beauty as much as on their outer one. Otherwise, those with a nasty personality would not be able to live up to their reputations built mainly by their great looks, and will probably end up in the same place in life no matter how much efforts they put into refining their outer beauty.

整體來說，我支持人們藉由醫美整型來提升自我信心，只要符合以安全為前提的原則。但另一方面來說，正如成語「名不符實」所形容的，人們應當也要以積極的態度，在內在美的提升上下功夫，要不然，儘管外表美好而人氣、名氣匯集，但內在個性差勁而名不符實的話，就算美如天仙，也無法改變人生中的處境。

1 教育

2 社會法律議題

3 民生生活

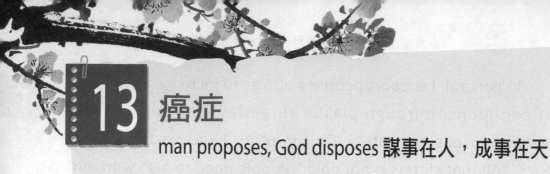

13 癌症

man proposes, God disposes 謀事在人，成事在天

成語閱讀故事

　　成語「謀事在人，成事在天」，其出處來自文學名著《三國演義》中，第一百零三回，描述到諸葛亮眼看原本精密的計畫，被突如其來的大雨所破壞，而感嘆「謀事在人，成事在天，不可強也。」其所形容的是，人可以有再多事先的計畫及謀略，但事情能不能按照其所安排的計畫來發展，很多時候都還是要看當下的機運，因為人生中有太多的變數了；在英文中，有句諺語「man proposes, God disposes」，說明很多時候，人們處心積慮地安排計畫，但最終人生中有太多的變數，所以並不是每件事都能按照計畫走，也就是成語「謀事在人，成事在天」的意思。

寫作題目

Around the globe, cancer is one of the leading causes of death in today's world. By definition, cancer refers to abnormal cell growth on a variety of human organs.

In fact, cancer is a kind of debilitating disease as it can often easily, if left untreated, spread and migrate to other body parts, and thus drastically worsen one's health condition in the blink of an eye.

Currently, there are a few choices when it comes to cancer treatment, such as chemotherapy and so on.

However, as much as the world as a whole is dedicating all available resources to finding the cure for cancer, there is still not a single fix that is one-hundred percent effective.

What is your view on the human battle against cancer? Please explain.

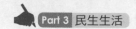

✚ 寫作技巧解析

　　題目說道，在世界各地，癌症是許多國家中人口死亡的主因，而癌症本身是個嚴重的病症，儘管世界各國正努力開發、研究各種癌症治療的方式，但還是無法開發出百分之百有效的療程；以下範文，對於人類與癌症病魔的對抗，採取「謀事在人，成事在天 man proposes, God disposes」的樂觀態度，認為儘管在對抗癌症的道路上，充滿了未知數，但若能夠樂觀以對、積極地籌畫治療，就能增加戰勝癌症及存活的機率。

⑥ 應試撇步

　　範文提到，自古以來人類「征服 conquer」了許多不可能的「壯舉 feats」，但在對抗癌症這方面，還未能找出可以百分之百治癒癌症的方法，而在各種對抗癌症的醫療方法中，「化療 chemotherapy」是比較常見的，但它的療程俱有「雙刃劍 double-edged sword」的效果，因為化療同時會毀滅癌細胞，以及正常、良性的細胞，也因有這麼多的變數，癌症病患在面對癌症這種「巨大、可畏的 formidable」的疾病時，需要以「謀事在人，成事在天 man proposes, God disposes」的心態來面對，才能得到「心靈的平靜 peace of mind」。

作文範例　　　🔘 MP3 046

Around the whole wide world, there are many things that had once been commonly deemed impossible, but had later been achieved and conquered by humankind. Unfortunately, cancer is not one of these conquered feats yet. As of now, people are still not presented with one solution or cure that is one-hundred percent effective when it comes to treating cancer. As a result, many patients facing cancer today have to learn how to hold a positive mindset. They have to learn how to accept the fact that all they can do in the situation is to give their best shot at this battle against cancer, and leave the rest to God. In other words, Today's cancer patients have to come to terms with the fact that all they can do is to remain positive and do not stop fighting, just as the saying "man proposes, God disposes" goes.

　　在這廣闊的世界，有許多事情都是曾經被認為不可能，但後來都被人類達成、征服了。很可惜的是，癌症的治癒還尚未是這些輝煌的成就之一，因為人類至今還未有一個能百分之百治癒癌症的療法，而也因為這樣，今日許多面對癌症的病患，必須學習如何抱持著一個正面的態度，並且學習接受在這樣的情況裡，他們能做的就是放手一搏，而學習接受之後病情的發展，是只能任由老天安排的；換句話說，今日的癌症病患，正如「謀事在人，成事在天」所說，必須學會如何接受，並不輕易放棄，堅強、持續與病魔奮鬥。

In terms of cancer treatments that are currently available, there are a variety of options. Among these options, chemotherapy is probably the most common one in practice, and this therapy is often considered to be the sort of double-edged sword treatment where not only cancer cells are destroyed through the treatment but also the normal, good ones. Because of the fact that too many uncontrollable variables at stake, cancer patients can sometimes be discouraged by the uncertainty of the treatment and eventually become depressed and pessimistic.

　以現有各式各樣的癌症治療法來説，化療也許是治療上最常見的，而其療效也常被認為俱有所謂的「雙刃劍」效果，因為化療不只毀滅癌症細胞，同一時間也對正常、良性的細胞造成衝擊，而因為有太多這些無法控制的變因，癌症病患有時會因療程的不確定性感到氣餒，進而對治療感到憂鬱、悲觀。

In conclusion, when it comes to the battle against cancer, it is important for cancer patients to embrace the mindset that things will work out the way as they are supposed to do. Only with this mentality can they have peace of mind in the face of this kind of formidable disease.

總結來說，在與癌症纏鬥時，癌症病患必須以船到橋頭自然直的心態來面對，這是很重要的，因為也只有這樣，他們在面對如此巨大、可畏的疾病時，才可能擁有心靈的平靜。

1 教育

2 社會法律議題

3 民生生活

國家圖書館出版品預行編目(CIP)資料

一次就考到雅思寫作6.5⁺ / Amanda Chou著
-- 初版. -- 新北市：倍斯特, 2020.02面；
公分. -- （考用英語系列；23）
ISBN 978-986-98079-3-7（平裝附光碟）
1.國際英語語文測試系統　　2.作文

805.189　　　　　　　　　　　109001380

考用英語系列 023

一次就考到雅思寫作6.5⁺（附英式發音MP3）

初　　版　　2020年2月
定　　價　　新台幣399元

作　　者　　柯志儒
出　　版　　倍斯特出版事業有限公司
發 行 人　　周瑞德
電　　話　　886-2-8245-6905
傳　　真　　886-2-2245-6398
地　　址　　23558 新北市中和區立業路83巷7號4樓
E - m a i l　　best.books.service@gmail.com
官　　網　　www.bestbookstw.com
總 編 輯　　齊心琇
特約編輯　　陳韋佑
封面構成　　高鍾琪
內頁構成　　菩薩蠻數位文化有限公司
印　　製　　大亞彩色印刷製版股份有限公司

港澳地區總經銷　　泛華發行代理有限公司
地　　址　　香港新界將軍澳工業邨駿昌街7號2樓
電　　話　　852-2798-2323
傳　　真　　852-3181-3973